I0547716

NETTIE McCORKLE and the Horse Race

By
Gus Brackett

Illustrations by
Don Gill

Twelve Baskets Book Publishing
Three Creek, Idaho

Twelve Baskets Book Publishing, LLC
54899 Crawfish Rd.
Rogerson ID 83302
www.badgerthurston.com
12bookbaskets@gmail.com

ISBN 978-0-9841876-5-2

All rights reserved. No part of this book may be reproduced or transmitted in any form, or by any means, electronic or mechanical, including photocopying, recording, or by any information storage and retrieval system, without permission in writing from the publisher.

Copyright 2020 Gus Brackett
All rights reserved
Printed in the U.S.A.

Author photo by Jill Davidson, Emotion Portrait Design
Edited by Dawn Geluso
Cover Design by Chantel Miller

Other books by Gus Brackett:
Badger Thurston and the Cattle Drive
Badger Thurston and the Runaway Stagecoach
Badger Thurston and the Mud Pits
Badger Thurston and the Trouble at the Rodeo

Table of Contents

Illustrations

Chapter One

NETTIE McCORKLE'S HEART RACES. Her mind races. Her eyes dart in all directions, taking quick snapshots of obstacles on the ground in front of her. A rock, root of a tree, gnarled sagebrush. Each poses a danger to Nettie and her racing horse.

The wind beats on Nettie's face, and a few stray hairs tickle her cheeks and neck with every stride from the little black horse she rides. Just ahead, a small ravine lies across her path. She hasn't time to stop, and she wouldn't anyway if she could. She squeezes tightly to the reins and braces herself.

The athletic horse jumps, and Nettie leans forward to keep up with the flying thoroughbred. A chill of excitement tingles up Nettie's spine. As Nettie and the little horse, Dixie, clear the shallow ravine, Nettie braces again, this time for impact. As her swift steed's front feet hit the ground, Nettie lurches forward. Her stomach spins at the jolt.

Nettie has fallen off her horse before at this speed and, boy, does it hurt.

It starts with a sharp pain that shocks her entire body. Her head immediately begins throbbing, and her lungs stop working. She gasps for air but just can't catch her breath. She has dust and dirt everywhere — in her mouth, up her nose, even down her pants.

Once she finally catches her breath, that's when the real pain starts. If something is broken, now she feels it. Even if nothing is broken, everything hurts. But the pain and, more precisely, the overwhelming fear add to the thrill of the race, the thrill of the speed as the trail is eaten up in front of her and Dixie.

In all her thirteen years, nothing scares Nettie more and nothing thrills her more than racing horses.

The Wilkerson Ranch sits about a mile down the creek from Nettie's place. Ms. Kat Wilkerson owns about 5,000 horses that roam the ranges. Dozens of cowboys work at her ranch.

Ms. Wilkerson's brother Jimmy Wilkerson spends most of his time riding the ranges tending to the horses. Her other brother, Sam Wilkerson, takes care of the money and the books at a tiny office in the city. But Ms. Wilkerson, a strong and refined woman, owns and manages the whole ranch.

With all her thousands of working horses, her most prized horses are a small herd of about twenty. These are her thoroughbred horses. These are her racehorses. And the best trainer in the area trains these racehorses, Mrs. Maggie Dickens.

Mrs. Dickens has been riding horses on these ranges since before the Wilkersons or any other pioneers came to this area. As a Shoshone, her love of horses is bone deep, and her skills are steeped in native tradition.

The Wilkerson Ranch used to be one of the largest in the West. More than 10,000 Wilkerson horses at one time roamed the ranges around the ranch. Every week, Wilkerson horses and mules were rounded up and trailed to the railroad depot 100 miles away, where they were loaded on dozens of rail cars and literally sent around the world, most of them sold to the U.S. and British cavalries.

In those days, Ms. Wilkerson used her varied charms to sell her horses. She traveled to San Francisco, Kansas City, Chicago, and New Orleans to meet with buyers of hundreds of horses.

She has impeccable taste, was trained at the West's best finishing school, and has a beauty about her that gives her a bargaining advantage over almost any man.

When the bicycle first gained popularity, Ms. Wilkerson told everyone who would listen that "the bicycle is barbaric and will never replace the horse."

And she was correct on that count.

However, the newfangled automobile is a threat to a ranch that sells horses. Even more critical, peace has broken out. The Americans and British are at peace with the rest of world, and major cavalries no longer need a steady supply of equines.

So the Wilkerson Ranch is now selling most of its horses to local cowboys. But the cowboys in the area don't need a constant supply of new horses, and they don't have the money an army has. So the Wilkerson Ranch still makes money, but not nearly as much as is in its heyday.

But all that doesn't matter to Nettie. She just wants to ride fast horses — and the more Nettie wins, the more she gets to ride.

These racehorses are the kind Nettie loves best.

Ms. Wilkerson needs a lightweight rider for her horses who can handle a half-ton of runaway horse. And Nettie needs a horse that will run fast. So Nettie and Ms. Wilkerson have forged a tenuous relationship.

Nettie rides Wilkerson racehorses and gets paid fifty cents per race. And Ms. Wilkerson wins 100 dollars in prize money every time Nettie wins first place.

Racing horses isn't just a fickle romance for Nettie. Some real work is involved. To develop a young horse's stamina and speed, the horse must be ridden every day. And that's what Nettie is doing today with Dixie.

Nettie sits astride 1,000 pounds of pure muscle. Every stride is a powerful lunge forward at forty miles per hour.

Nettie grips her reins securely but gently. In the fury of the speed, she makes minor adjustments to the horse's track by tugging gently on the reins. Nettie's riding genius is her ability to maintain her soft hands despite the adrenaline coursing through her body.

Nettie's braided long red hair is tucked neatly beneath a gray riding hat and flows rhythmically with every stride of her horse. She wears gloves with beaded fringe and tall black boots. Unlike all the other girls, Nettie wears baggy pants instead of a dress.

On this perfectly calm spring morning, the wind speeds over Nettie's face. The front of her cowboy hat tips up like a Pony Express rider. Nettie's eyes are wide open, and she breaths rapidly as the little black horse eats up the trail in front of them. With the exhilaration of the ride, Nettie still uses gentle moves to guide her powerful horse.

As Nettie and Dixie ride through the bottom of a wide canyon, the trail winds through a narrow patch of willows.

Without warning, Dixie falls to her knees.

Nettie instantly turns her toes out to bind herself to the saddle. She grips more tightly with her knees and thighs as her normally surefooted horse skids nearly thirty feet.

Nettie lifts on her reins, both to stop her horse and keep her backside in the saddle. As Dixie comes to an abrupt stop, Nettie nearly flies out of the saddle. A less experienced rider would be writhing in pain on the ground right now, but Nettie has learned how to ride out a stumble.

As the horse comes to a stop, Nettie quickly swings off to assess any damage. She runs her hands over the front feet of her horse. Dixie's knees are scraped but not bleeding. Lower on Dixie's left ankle, Nettie notices a narrow scrape — a clue perhaps. Nettie quickly walks back up the trail to where Dixie tripped.

At the exact spot where Dixie tripped, a rope of braided rawhide stretches between two sturdy aspen trees.

Nettie's eye narrow.

Otis Gregerson, Nettie thinks. Nettie's blood boils. *That twerp put this rope up to purposely trip my horse!*

She unties the rope and heads back to Dixie.

Otis Gregerson rides Mercury, and they always win the spring horse race. Otis, while little in size, is a big bully, matched only by his big bullying gray stallion.

Otis plays pranks on all the other jockeys. He once put horse manure in one jockey's boots and shortened another's stirrups when he wasn't looking.

But this goes well beyond a prank. Dixie and Nettie both could have been seriously injured.

Nettie wraps the rope around her saddle horn, remounts Dixie, and rides more gently the remaining half-mile of her exercise run.

Dixie runs easily through the gate at the Wilkerson Ranch and around the yard. The athletic black horse is covered with sweat. There is a bit of foam around the saddle, and Dixie is frothing at the mouth.

Nettie pulls the reins tight, and the horse reluctantly slows to a walk. Nettie and her horse walk anxiously to the horse barn. The teen dismounts and leads the horse through a gate. At the barn, she quickly pulls off the saddle and stores it.

Nettie walks the black horse to a smaller round corral, strips off the halter, and stands in the middle of the corral as the horse walks in circles around her. The young jockey fumes at Otis and watches Dixie's front leg as she walks.

As she works, two women approach.

"Good afternoon, Nettie," a refined woman says. Ms. Wilkerson wears a long black skirt, fitted black jacket with bright silver buttons, and a white blouse with a bit of lace peeking out the front. Her hair is swept back into a fancy bun with tight curls framing her face. She wears expensive pearl earrings. Not a stitch or thread is out of place.

"Howdy, Ms. Wilkerson," Nettie replies. Ms. Wilkerson cringes with the "howdy" greeting.

"Howdy, Mrs. Dickens," Nettie says to the horse trainer, the less formal of the pair.

The presence of the two older women calms Nettie's anger.

"Howdy," Mrs. Dickens replies with a tip of her hat. She has a stoic frown on her face — not because she is angry or sad, but because that's just how her face is. Nettie is sure she was born with the frown.

"How did my horse run today?" Ms. Wilkerson asks. She speaks quickly and carefully enunciates every word.

"Steady," Nettie replies. The teen gets in trouble if she says "fast." She also gets in trouble if she says "slow." So she has learned to reply "steady" regardless of how the black colt runs.

"Open her up a lil' bit more next time," Mrs. Dickens says. She speaks slowly and all her words seem to lean on one another.

"I will," she agrees, because Nettie rides Dixie as fast as she will go every time.

The black colt walks in circles around Nettie as the conversation continues.

Mrs. Dickens peers between the fourth and fifth poles. Her dirty black hat folds easily as she presses her forehead against the fence. Her hat has a beaded hat band and an eagle feather tucked between the band and the crown. Her tawny fingers grasp the rough fence. Her pants are almost identical to Nettie's, baggy and brown. And her shirt is a bright red pattern partially covered by a brown vest embellished with beads and porcupine quills. Her black and gray braids fall loosely from both sides of her hat.

"Dixie's limpin'," Mrs. Dickens says without emotion.

"She is what!" Ms. Wilkerson cries. For the first time in months, Ms. Wilkerson looks slightly improper.

"Now, she's not truly damaged," Mrs. Dickens reassures. "She's just a lil' sore on that front right. It's barely noticeable, but we have to keep an eye on it."

Ms. Wilkerson's face turns red. "Have you been running my horse too fast again?"

"Just steady," Nettie says, knowing that saying the right thing at this point is critical. "Dixie tripped on this," Nettie says as she unwraps the rawhide rope from the horn of her saddle. "It was stretched across the trail where I was ridin'. It must have been Otis Gregerson."

Ms. Wilkerson tips her chin and raises an eyebrow. Her skepticism is obvious, and she has reason to be skeptical.

Nettie has been taught that honesty is a virtue, and she tries to be honest. Her teacher at school would say she's honest, and the owners at the Three Creek Store would vouch for her honesty. Nettie is known as an honest girl — with one exception.

When it comes to riding horses, Nettie will say anything to stay in the saddle — even if that means tiptoeing around the truth from time to time. Ms. Wilkerson has noticed these previous lapses of truth.

"Do you have any proof?" Ms. Wilkerson asks. A glint of light reflects off her silver broach and into Nettie's eyes. The teen squints, making her look even more like she's lying.

"I only found this rope tied between two trees," Nettie pleads.

"Avoid the trees."

"Yes, ma'am," Nettie says, lowering her eyes to the ground.

"This black colt is the best chance we have at winning the spring derby. I will find another rider if you make my stock lame."

"Who?" Nettie asks.

"Pardon me?" Ms. Wilkerson replies. Her head recoils and her eyes widen.

"Who else?" Nettie asks, equally indignant. "Where else can ya find someone of my small size and ridin' ability?"

"It would be a detriment to feel too safe in your position, young lady! I will find someone else if I must."

Ms. Wilkerson spins on her heel, pulls the front of her long skirt up slightly, and shuffles back to her house. The pleats in her velvety black skirt whip about her, and the folds in the back swish back and forth with every step like a horse's tail.

With the deliberate movement, a few stray hairs fall from her previously perfect fancy woven bun. Even in her everyday clothes, she wears more silver than a Spanish vaquero.

"Don't worry 'bout Ms. Wilkerson," Mrs. Dickens says in her slow and measured voice. "I'll calm her down. But go easy on Dixie tomorrow. Just stick to the flats, and don't run her hard."

"I'll keep her checked up," Nettie says, again saying exactly what the trainer wants to hear. "Did ya remember my pay, Mrs. Dickens?"

"I left a nickel with your rig in the barn," Mrs. Dickens replies. "And don't spend it all on cinnamon sticks. A few more pounds, and you'll weigh just as much as the boys. And then ya really would be replaceable."

"No cinnamon sticks," Nettie replies with her fingers crossed behind her back.

IT IS AN EASY one-mile walk from the Wilkerson Ranch to the McCorkle Place. It's a half-mile past that to the Three Creek Store. Nettie enthusiastically walks the extra distance to spend her recently acquired coin.

The Three Creek Store is a simple rock building with two freshly constructed rooms on the north end that serve as living quarters.

A few miners linger at the store. Some are fresh faced with empty pockets and optimism as they head to the mines in Jarbidge. Others are haggard and dirty, pessimistically headed home from the mines in Jarbidge with their pockets equally empty.

The Three Creek Store is on the road to this freshly minted mining town.

Three Creek is a small town. In fact, it isn't really even a town. It boasts a store, couple barns, and hotel, as well as a few hawks, ground squirrels, a family of badgers, and not much else.

Mr. Joel Reed and his wife, Eliza, own the store. Mr. Reed is a slight man. His brown hair is matted on his head like a helmet. He has tiny eyes that look even smaller behind his wire-rimmed glasses. He wears a blue striped shirt with overalls and an apron.

Mr. Reed stands behind a long counter full of jars of candy and other sundry items. The store has multiple bins of dry goods, including flour, sugar, and coffee. Canned goods, such as peaches, meat, and green beans, fill a set of shelves.

"Good afternoon, Ms. McCorkle," Mr. Reed says softly, his voice an octave higher than most men. "Can I get your cinnamon sticks?"

"Yes, sir. And a handful of gumdrops, please," Nettie says. She always gets gumdrops after a hard day. She buys cinnamon sticks every day.

"That'll be three cents," Mr. Reed says as he places the candy on a sheet of wax paper and rolls it all neatly together.

She hands her nickel to Mr. Reed, and he hands her the bundle and two cents.

"Thank you, Mr. Reed," Nettie says.

"Come again soon," he replies as Nettie steps out the door.

A covered porch wraps around the front and sides of the store. A steep canyon wall presses near its back wall. The rock store fits in with the rocky landscape around it. A creek flows lazily through the narrow valley, and narrow hay fields flank it. A road runs down the valley and past the store.

Before the door can close behind her, Nettie tears into her candy and shoves a chunk of cinnamon stick into her mouth. She looks up and sees a family of four approaching.

Two girls wear matching light blue dresses with ribbons in their hair. The younger skips and whistles as she trails behind a man and woman, her parents, Nettie assumes. The older girl plods far behind the others, keeping her head tucked.

Nettie guesses the older girl is about her age.

Nettie lights up, skips down the stairs to her, and asks, "Ya new here?"

"Yes."

"Where'd ya come from?" Nettie asks.

"Missouri," the girl says without looking up.

"Missouri," Nettie says. "I guess it could be worse. Ya could've come from Arkansas."

The girl looks up and notices Nettie smiling.

Nettie's smile persists, waiting for the new girl to get the joke. Nettie's smile fades as she realizes no laugh is coming.

"So what's your name?" Nettie asks.

"Bertha Jo Stillwell."

"Bertha Jo, huh?" Nettie repeats. "I don't think I like your name."

"I'm sorry, I guess," the girl replies, looking at the ground again.

"Don't be sorry," Nettie says. "It's not your fault. You're just stuck with it. Do ya have a nickname?"

The girl looks at Nettie. "My uncle calls me Bert."

"Bert, huh?" Nettie says as she walks around the girl, sizing her up. "That sounds like a boy's name. How 'bout Birdie?"

"I guess," the girl says dully. "I kind of like Bertha Jo. But if ya don't like it, ya can call me Birdie."

"That's good," Nettie says. She pulls a cinnamon stick out of the folded paper and hands it to her new friend, Birdie.

"Ya wanna cinnamon stick?" Nettie asks.

"I don't really like sweets, but I'll take one — to be polite," Birdie says, reaching out and snatching the cinnamon stick before Nettie can pull it away.

"Whattaya like to do?" Nettie asks.

"I don't know," Birdie says, shrugging her shoulders and spinning the cinnamon around her tongue. "I've never lived in an area that has a girl my age. I mostly clean, cook, and help my mom around the house."

"Do ya like to ride horses?" Nettie asks. "I love to ride horses, and I'd love to have someone to ride with."

"My dad taught me how to ride," Birdie replies, "but I haven't ridden in 'bout a year."

"Let's go for a ride tomorrow," Nettie says.

"I don't know. I'd have to ask my parents," Birdie says without looking up. "I doubt they'll let me go."

"Mrs. Stillwell," Nettie sings out. Mrs. Stillwell looks back at Nettie. "Can Bertha Jo go for a ride with me tomorrow?"

"Yes, of course," Mrs. Stillwell says. Birdie glares at her mother. "It would do her some good to go out with a friend."

"I don't know—" Birdie starts.

"It's settled then," Nettie interrupts. "Meet me at the Wilkerson Ranch at seven."

"In the mornin'?" Birdie cries.

"Seven o'clock sharp, and don't be late."

Nettie skips away, sucking on a cinnamon stick.

"See ya tomorrow," Nettie yells without looking back.

"See ya then," Birdie replies unenthusiastically.

Chapter Two

THE SMELL OF A barn. Nettie pulls the distinctive smell into her nostrils. It smells musky, like sweat and horse poop and leather. The cedar planks add to the aroma. City people might say it smells gross. But to a country girl like Nettie, the scent is intoxicating.

Nettie has two horses saddled, the little black she usually rides and a bay the Wilkersons rent out to children and the elderly. As Nettie slides the latigoes through the D-rings of the saddle, Birdie walks in.

"Hey, Birdie," Nettie says.

"Hey," Birdie replies, plunging her hands into the pockets of her too-big wool pants. Her shirt is too big also, and her hat looks like it's just been pulled out of a trunk.

"Ya don't look very excited to be here," Nettie says.

"I don't really know what I'm doin' here," Birdie says with a sigh. "I should be at home helpin' my mom."

"That's the nice part 'bout a dirty house," Nettie slaps her thigh. "It'll still be there waitin' for ya when ya get done ridin'!" She chortles. "You'll have fun. Taylor is a great horse to ride."

Birdie rolls her eyes. "Will he buck me off?"

"Taylor is dog-broke gentle," Nettie reassures. "He couldn't buck off a wet saddle blanket."

"So I'm ridin' a slow, ol' nag?"

"Taylor's not slow. Ms. Wilkerson only has fast horses."

"Not too fast," Birdie says. "I'm not *that* good of a rider."

"Er, you'll do just fine," Nettie replies with a raised eyebrow.

Nettie unhitches the horses and walks the two out of the barn. She hands Taylor's reins to Birdie, who sizes up the massive horse.

"Loop the reins around his neck," Nettie tells Birdie.

"I know. I *knooow!*" Birdie leans forward, hands on hips. "I've done this before."

Nettie steps back, her eyebrows reaching for her hairline. Then she pivots on her heels and swings onto Dixie's back.

Birdie circles Taylor twice, measures his reins, and checks his cinch.

"He's all ready to go," Nettie says with exasperation. "All ya have to do is jump on."

Birdie narrows her eyes and whips her braid around as she turns her back to Nettie. Birdie sticks her boot into the stirrup and swings onto the back of the big bay horse.

"Walk him around the yard a couple times," Nettie commands. "I can show ya a thing or two 'bout how to ride."

"I already know how to ride," Birdie says. "My dad taught me on his plow horse."

Birdie sits tall in the saddle. She holds the reins gently and low against her horse's neck. She sits with her heels down and toes turned out. She kicks Taylor, and the two trot around the yard.

She's not too bad a rider, Nettie thinks. *Most first-time riders bounce awkwardly in the saddle when they trot, lookin' like a sack of flour tied loosely to a packsaddle. But not Birdie. She posts comfortably up and down like a classically trained English-style rider.*

The newcomer gently taps her heels on Taylor's ribs, and the horse dutifully gallops in a tight circle. She holds her hands low and uses subtle cues to guide him.

"You're a pretty good rider," Nettie says, watching from atop her perch.

"I've told ya several times," Birdie huffs, "I know how to ride."

"Then why didn't ya wanna go ridin' with me?"

"Well, just because I'm good at it doesn't mean I like ridin'."

"How can ya not like ridin'?" The thought is so contrary to Nettie that she can't understand. *That's like not likin' breathin' or eatin,'* she thinks, her jaw falling open.

"Are we just ridin' in circles, or are we gonna go out and 'bout?" Birdie asks.

"We'll head out on a trail," Nettie says.

"Let's get at it," Birdie says. "I've got other things to do today."

"Follow me," Nettie huffs as she pulls the black horse around.

Nettie and Dixie lead Birdie and Taylor out the front gate. Nettie pulls back on the reins to slow her horse while in view of the Wilkerson Ranch, remembering her admonishment from the day before to keep her speed under control.

17

The four wind up a trail that tops the narrow valley and leads to a wide-open flat. Nettie looks behind her. To the young jockey's surprise, Birdie trails closely behind.

On the flat, Nettie lets Dixie's reins loose to show Birdie what a fast racehorse looks like.

Nettie reaches her arms forward to slack the reins. She kicks Dixie three times to ask a little bit more speed. Nettie's heart jumps into her throat as the hard ground and unforgiving rocks sail past perilously close beneath them. Both Nettie and Dixie breathe hard as the little racehorse points her nose out like a hunting dog and flies easily across the flat.

As the flat rises slightly, Nettie pulls back on the horse's reins. Dixie resists before hopping a couple times and slowing to a jog.

Nettie inhales deeply and looks behind her to see how far back Birdie and Taylor are. To Nettie's surprise, the two are right on their heels. The young jockey pulls back again, and her horse stops. Birdie and Taylor circle around Nettie and stop.

"You're doin' a good job keepin' up," Nettie says.

"Ya sound surprised," Birdie replies. "I thought ya said Taylor was a fast horse."

"He is."

"So ya didn't think *I* could keep up," Birdie replies flatly, trapping Nettie in a logical quandary.

"I, uh, I didn't know what to expect," Nettie says, trying to wiggle out. "I haven't really gone that fast yet."

"Why don't ya run her fast?" Birdie asks as her chin drops and her head waggles. "I know my way back. Don't worry 'bout me."

"It's not that." Nettie knows Birdie is goading her into riding faster — and Nettie typically doesn't need much prompting. "I have to keep a good pace with Dixie. I'm just tryin' to exercise her. I'm not racin' her today."

"Okay," Birdie says. "I guess that makes sense."

"We better keep movin'," Nettie says with a gentle tug on the inside rein.

"I'm just followin' ya," Birdie says.

Fine. Then try to keep up with this! Nettie huffs. *I'll show ya what a racehorse really looks like.*

And Nettie and Dixie take off like a lightning strike. The sagebrush lining the trail smacks Nettie's shins. But with adrenaline coursing through her veins, she barely notices. Nettie clinches the slacked reins tightly and squeezes her legs to the saddle to stay in the seat. Dixie jumps a rock that lies across the trail, and Nettie's backside leaves the saddle but settles back down before she is thrown. She swallows her fear and races forward.

With one more flat before they return to the ranch, Nettie slacks the reins and kicks her horse three times. Dixie pins her ears back and pounds across the plain, kicking up a rooster tail of dust.

As Nettie gets within sight of the ranch, she sees Ms. Wilkerson and Mrs. Dickens standing in the front gate with their arms folded.

Nettie pulls back on the reins to slow Dixie. The black colt is soaked with sweat and panting like an overheated hound dog. Nettie pulls on the reins again and slows to a walk, hoping the black will catch her breath before they reach the front gate.

Nettie looks behind her to search for Birdie. To her surprise, Birdie casually pulls up right behind them.

As Nettie walks Dixie toward the gate, she notices the young horse limping slightly on her front left hoof. Nettie quickly climbs off and picks up the front hoof.

She feels first the ankle and then the cannon bone just above the ankle. The bone isn't swollen, but it is hot. Sweat from the black's chest and legs gets all over Nettie, making the exertion even more obvious. Dixie's nostrils flare, her eyes are wide open and glassy, and her ears are perked forward.

"Easy, girl," Nettie says, petting the horse's neck.

"Is everythin' all right?" Birdie asks, seeing the concern on Nettie's face.

"Her front leg is a lil' sore," Nettie says, narrowing her eyes at Birdie. "Why did ya push me so hard?"

"What!" Birdie exclaims. "Ya told me to keep up. I followed directions. If ya rode her too fast, you're the one who didn't follow directions."

Nettie looks away. Her mind races for a witty rebuttal, but Birdie is obviously right.

I don't like my new friend, Nettie seethes.

The young jockey leads Dixie over to the adults, a fake, brittle smile pasted on her face. Birdie and Taylor follow behind.

Why do Birdie and Taylor look like they've been on a picnic while my horse is lame and my hair feels like I walked through a tornado? Nettie wonders as she tries to smooth her braid.

"She's turned up lame," Mrs. Dickens says, walking to Dixie. She reaches down and pulls up the sore hoof like a farrier. She feels the ankle and cannon bone.

"Cannon bone's pretty hot," she says. "She's not favorin' it much but enough I can tell."

"Have you been running my horse too hard again, Nettie?" Ms. Wilkerson asks.

"I took her for an easy run," Nettie protests, "just like ya said."

"Then why is she breathing hard, and why is she covered in sweat?"

"It's a pretty hot day," Nettie replies. "Maybe that's why her cannon bone is warm."

"It's only hot if you've been runnin' too fast," Mrs. Dickens says.

"I am getting someone else to ride my racehorse," Ms. Wilkerson says.

"But all the boys around here are too heavy for Dixie," Nettie says, struggling to keep her job.

"With as many cinnamon sticks as you have been sneaking, you are almost as heavy as a boy," Ms. Wilkerson sneers. Her words bite even more because of their truth.

"You there, miss, what is your name?" Ms. Wilkerson asks Birdie as she dismounts.

Birdie tepidly looks up. She looks to her left and to her right, hoping Ms. Wilkerson is talking to someone else. But there is no one else.

Her eyes flicker like a treed mountain lion, her scrunched face showing her displeasure. Birdie was perfectly content sitting in the background far away from the uncomfortable argument. Now in the spotlight, she folds her arms and points her head toward the ground.

"I'm nobody," Birdie replies. She clutches her arms more tightly to herself. "I really don't wanna be here."

"Oh, nonsense," Ms. Wilkerson scoffs. "The modern woman must always be prepared to give voice to her opinions."

Birdie gulps.

"My name is Bertha Jo Stillwell, ma'am, but Nettie calls me Birdie," the girls says. She glances up to be polite, and then looks down again.

"Could you ride my racehorse on the same route you did today?"

"Yes, ma'am, I could, perhaps with some help. But I don't like to ride fast." Birdie slowly looks up.

"Too fast is the cause of our present situation. I prefer you ride Dixie more slowly. I will pay you a nickel a day."

"I don't think so," Birdie says. "I have too much to do at home."

"A dime for every day," Ms. Wilkerson negotiates.

"I really don't—"

"Fifteen cents per day," Ms. Wilkerson says. "Do not be a fool. Take my offer."

"Okay. I'll ride your horse."

Nettie's mouth falls open. She wants to protest, but no words escape her lips.

"Nettie, you will ride Taylor to show the way," Ms. Wilkerson commands.

"For fifteen cents per day?" Nettie asks.

"For three cents per day," Ms. Wilkerson replies. "I am the only one with racehorses in the area who will let girls ride. Without me, you have no way to ride fast horses."

Nettie stands silently. *I'm in no position to negotiate. I can't just walk away.* She sighs and hangs her head.

"Be here bright and early tomorrow," Ms. Wilkerson demands of the girls. "Ride before it gets too hot."

"Yes, ma'am," both girls reply sourly.

Nettie aims an evil glance at Birdie, who doesn't notice, annoying Nettie even more.

Nettie unwinds the latigoes and pulls the saddles from Taylor and then Dixie. She angrily hands a brush to Birdie, who grabs it, huffs, and turns to Taylor to brush him off.

The two teens refuse to look at each other and work in silence. After brushing Dixie, Nettie grabs a pitchfork and walks into a stall. She stabs the pitchfork into horse manure and slings it to the front of the barn.

The horse apples fly dangerously close to Birdie's feet. Nettie isn't intentionally trying to toss horse poop on Birdie's boots, but she makes little effort to avoid the newcomer.

Nettie grabs Dixie's reins and leads her into her stall. Birdie follows Nettie's lead and guides Taylor into the other empty stall.

Nettie grabs the pitchfork again and flings hay into the manger — and Birdie's hair.

And so Nettie's workday ends.

Nettie started the day as the jockey for the Wilkerson Ranch. And now she's been demoted to groom.

And it's all because of her new "friend," Birdie.

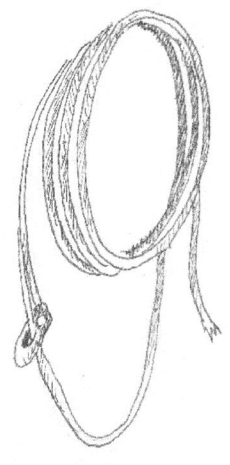

Chapter Three

NETTIE GOES STRAIGHT HOME, skipping cinnamon sticks today. Her stomach is in knots, and her head is pounding from the stress of the day. She arrives to the normal chaos of the McCorkle household.

Her father is using his favorite tool, a three-pound hammer, to fix his hay rake, which is larger than a hand rake and pulled by two horses. Old Man McCorkle uses the rake to pull cut hay into piles.

Nettie is certain the only thing her father is accomplishing is venting frustration over his broken rake.

Her younger sister, Melly, swings on a wooden board tied to a beam in the barn. She sings loudly. Melly subscribes to the Sunday school teacher philosophy of, "If ya can't sing good, sing loud." The song sounds a little bit like "Hot Cross Buns" — but horribly out of tune and with jumbled lyrics.

Her younger brother is playing with his favorite toy, a small animal. This time, it's a cat. He sneaks up to one of the barn cats and stomps on its tail. The cat shrieks an awful *MEOWWWW* and jumps in the air.

Nettie secretly wishes the cat would scratch her mischievous brother.

Her mother darts about the house. It seems like she is doing dishes, laundry, cooking dinner, and sweeping the floors all at the same time. Nettie has an urge to help her busy mother. But she takes a deep breath, exhales, and the urge passes.

Nettie walks into her room, flops on her bed, and buries her face in her pillow, wanting to cry. A knock on the front door interrupts her pity party. A few seconds later, her mother peeks in.

"Nettie, your friend, Birdie, is here," Mrs. McCorkle says.

"She's not my friend."

"Oh, nonsense," Her mother snaps. "Ya went ridin' with her today."

"Well, I don't wanna see her," Nettie pouts into her pillow.

"Don't be a brat," Mrs. McCorkle says as she lowers her chin and raises her eyebrows. "Get out here and see her."

Nettie grudgingly sulks out of her small, dimly lit room.

Birdie stands uncomfortably on the front porch. Nettie walks past her and sits on the front step.

"Hey, Nettie," Birdie says.

Nettie does not reply.

"I just wanna say I'm sorry."

Nettie perks up slightly. *Ya should be sorry,* Nettie thinks. But prudence holds her tongue. As the only other girl in the area, Nettie likes the idea of a friend. She just hasn't warmed to the idea that it has to be Birdie.

"I didn't ask for the job," Birdie continues. "I really don't want it. I didn't even wanna go ridin' this mornin'."

"So you're quittin'?" Nettie asks.

"No," Birdie replies. "Ms. Wilkerson is offerin' too much money. And besides that, she sees somethin' in me that maybe I don't even see in myself."

It's all 'bout the money, Nettie pouts, rolling her eyes at her greedy friend. *I would ride a fast horse for free.*

"So, you're just in it for the money," Nettie sneers. "Do ya even enjoy ridin'?"

"I don't know. There's a long list of things I'd rather be doin', and a longer list of people I'd rather be with," Birdie replies, with her shoulders slumped and her head bowed. "But ridin' is okay."

Birdie's apathy annoys Nettie more than Birdie stealing her job. It's difficult to relate to someone who doesn't love riding horses. In the moment, Nettie almost likes Otis better. Granted, he does all the annoying boy things — throwing reptiles, rodents, and bugs at girls; slinging all types of poop at random people; pulling hair; and singing exasperating songs. But at least he has the good sense to like riding horses.

"I just wanted to say I'm sorry," Birdie huffs. She takes a deep, calming breath. "And I hope ya come ridin' tomorrow."

"Ya don't think ya can get Dixie rode without me," Nettie says, arrogantly nodding her head.

"It's not that at all!" Birdie cries. "I'm a better rider than ya give me credit for!"

Nettie wants to throw out a witty reply, but she can't think of anything. So she sits silently and picks at a knot on a nearby wooden slat. The silence stretches uncomfortably.

Why doesn't Birdie just leave? Nettie wonders. Nettie squirms on the front step without looking at Birdie.

"Well, I better get home," Birdie says. "I still hope you'll come ridin' tomorrow."

"I'll be there," Nettie snaps. "I have a job to do."

"NETTIE, MELLY, BUCKET!" MRS. McCorkle yells. "It's time to wash for dinner."

Bucket comes running from the yard, and all the cats sigh in relief. Melly jumps off the swing and stops singing, relieving everyone's ears. Nettie's father saunters into the house. Dinnertime is about the only time he isn't grouchy. Nettie is already sitting at the table, still bristling with anger.

Mrs. McCorkle carefully carries a cast-iron skillet toward them. The browned meat simmers next to the tender chunks of potatoes, and a pleasant-smelling steam fills the room.

"Set the plates," Mr. McCorkle commands.

His children jump to attention, and five plates are placed neatly around the table. Mr. McCorkle, as head of the household, doesn't help with the menial chores but watches for any imperfections in his home.

The children sit, Mrs. McCorkle sets the steaming pan on a cloth on the table, and, finally, with some regal pomp, Mr. McCorkle takes his throne. He ladles a portion of the stew onto his plate first and then meters out smaller portions to his children and then the largest portion to his wife.

The children fold their hands as Mr. McCorkle prays, "Lord, bless this food. In Jesus's name, amen."

As the last echo of "amen" fades into the evening, the kids slurp at their meal.

Mr. McCorkle, taking a full accounting of the happenings in his kingdom, asks the children about their day. "Melly, let's start with ya. Did ya practice your singin' today?"

"Yes, Daddy. I think I sang the song perfectly today."

Nettie chokes. *Only Melly's delusion is worse than her tone deafness.*

"How 'bout ya, Bucket? Did ya kill anythin' unnecessarily today?"

"I didn't kill anythin'. I just played with the cats. I was gonna kill a chicken. But Mom decided on stew for dinner instead of chicken pot pie."

"Ya remember what we talked 'bout?" Mr. McCorkle asks. "Only kill a chicken at your mother's promptin'."

"Yes, sir," Bucket says.

Nettie rolls her eyes. Her evil brother has no self-control.

"I see those eye rolls, Nettie," Mr. McCorkle says.

She rolls her eyes again.

"Well, tell me 'bout your day."

"I had a terrible day," Nettie exclaims.

"I doubt the drama," Mr. McCorkle says confidently. "It can't be that bad. What happened?"

"I lost my job," Nettie says.

"How? They won't find anyone else who can ride as well as ya."

"That's what I thought," Nettie says, exasperated. "But it turns out my new friend is a pretty good rider."

"Who is this *boy*?" Mr. McCorkle asks with panic in his voice. "And whatcha doin' bein' friendly with him!" The overprotective Mr. McCorkle looks both scared and pretty mad.

"Calm down, Dad," Nettie reassures her father. "Her name is Birdie."

"So, not a boy," Mr. McCorkle says with a relaxing sigh.

"Can we focus on my problem?" Nettie asks.

"Sure, sure. Go ahead."

"So I took her ridin' today, and at the end of the ride, Ms. Wilkerson offered my job to Birdie."

"Ah, I see," Mr. McCorkle says. "I didn't think Ms. Wilkerson could find a boy lighter than ya."

"Well, that's the problem," Nettie says. "She's lighter than me, and she's a pretty good rider."

"Well, just lose a lil' weight," Mr. McCorkle says. "Lay off your cinnamon sticks for a few weeks."

Nettie glares at her father.

"I know the struggle in bein' light enough to ride a racehorse," Mr. McCorkle's words trail off as he wistfully reflects on his glory days. "Remember, I was a jockey when I was a bit younger than ya. But then I had a growth spurt. And I've never seen a six-foot-two, hundred-and-eighty-pound jockey. I'm just sayin', ya have the frame to be a jockey, and—" Her father finally spots the glare and changes approaches.

"You're sure that's all there is to it?" Mr. McCorkle asks.

"Well," Nettie bites her lip and hesitates. "It might be that I rode Dixie a lil' bit too hard."

"A lil' too hard? How do ya know ya rode her too hard?"

"Mrs. Dickens seems to think I rode her a lil' bit too hard," Nettie replies, unable to look her father in the eye.

"What might give her that idea?"

"I'm guessin' it was because the lil' black was limpin' just a lil' bit when I got back," Nettie says.

"There's a lot of things that can make a horse limp," Mr. McCorkle says, struggling to give Nettie an out. "Ya didn't run her too hard, did ya?"

"Maybe just a lil' bit," Nettie says. "But it was all Birdie's fault."

"This girl who supposedly took your job from ya?" Mr. McCorkle asks. "How did she make ya run too fast?"

"She was keepin' up!" Nettie flaps her arms like a chicken hawk. "She's not a jockey, and she was keepin' up with me! I can't allow that."

"She might not have been a jockey," Mr. McCorkle says. "But because ya couldn't control yourself, she's a jockey now."

Nettie silently stares at her full plate. She hates it when her father is right.

"So what should I do?" Nettie asks. "Ms. Wilkerson will let me be a groom."

Her father slurps a spoonful of stew and chews for a while. Nettie assumes he is struggling for an answer, but in reality, he's struggling with a chunk of gristly fat.

"Ya need to go to work," Mr. McCorkle says. "Be the best groom ya can be. Ya keep workin' hard every day and do everythin' Ms. Wilkerson says, and I'm sure you'll have a job."

"But I don't want just a job," Nettie says. "I wanna race fast horses. I mean, the money is nice, but that's not why I'm doin' it."

"Then keep showin' up," Mr. McCorkle says. "There's always a job for someone who shows up and works hard."

"I will, Daddy," Nettie says as she walks to her father and hugs his neck.

Nettie grabs her and her father's plates and marches to the kitchen. She hastily washes the plates and returns them to the cabinet. Nettie would normally have other chores, but being the jockey in the McCorkle family comes with many privileges.

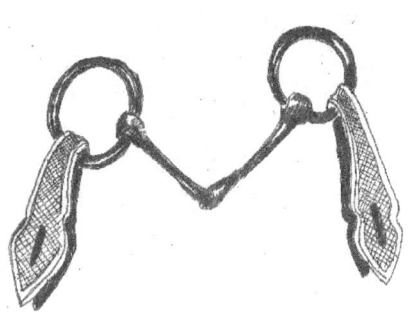

Chapter Four

THE DAWNING MORNING IS beautiful. Streaks of purple, orange, and pink reflect off the feathery clouds. A few twinkling stars linger as the last of the night creatures bed down. But Nettie doesn't notice.

The teen is a little annoyed. She woke up extra early so she would be the first one to the stable. But she arrives to find Birdie already brushing Dixie.

"Good mornin', Nettie," Birdie says quietly.

"Hurmph," Nettie replies.

She walks quickly into the tack room and reemerges with a bridle. With quick, familiar moves, she catches Taylor and throws a saddle on his back. She threads the cinch through the D-rings and pulls the saddle tight to Taylor's back. Nettie leads Taylor out of the horse barn and walks him in circles.

"Are ya gonna get your horse saddled?" Nettie asks.

"I'm not sure I can get her saddled right," Birdie says. "I've never really saddled a horse before."

Nettie shakes her head. *I could saddle Dixie without tightenin' the cinch so Birdie falls off. That's what she deserves,* Nettie thinks. But then her dad's advice returns to her. *He's right. I should just work hard and keep comin' back.*

She throws the saddle on Dixie and tightens the cinch properly.

"Do ya know how to warm up a horse?" Nettie asks.

"I've never really ridden anythin' that needed warmin' up," Birdie says. "I've never really been on a young horse."

Again, evil thoughts dance through Nettie's head. *I don't know what happened, Ms. Wilkerson,* Nettie rehearses silently. *Dixie just started buckin' for no apparent reason. That's what happens when ya put an inexperienced rider on a fast horse.*

She grins like a coyote but resists the temptation.

"Just bring her into the round pen," Nettie explains. "Make her walk and then run in a circle around ya."

"Can ya do it?" Birdie asks.

"I can. But if you're gonna be ridin' Dixie, she needs to get used to ya," Nettie says as she returns to Taylor. "Make sure she watches ya. She needs to respect ya, and makin' her watch ya is the easiest way to get her to respect ya."

"I just walk her around?" Birdie asks.

"Start her out at a walk, then trot, and then run just a bit," Nettie says.

Both girls circle the horses to warm them up. The horses don't breathe hard and barely break a sweat. Birdie is tentative and her movements lack authority. Nettie's actions are more confident, and she clearly knows what she's doing.

After about twenty minutes, Ms. Wilkerson and Mrs. Dickens stroll out of the ranch house. They move slower than rattlesnakes on a cold morning, their heads tilted toward each other, worry lining their faces.

Nettie has seen this before. Their discussions are never heated, but a hundred decisions a day need to be resolved on a horse ranch like theirs, especially in the spring when much of the work occurs despite having few horse sales.

The prize money from the spring derby might be the only money that comes into their coffers for months.

"Good morning, Birdie," Ms. Wilkerson says. "Good morning, Nettie."

Birdie and Nettie sing together, "Good mornin', Ms. Wilkerson."

Birdie's sandy blonde hair is braided in pigtails. Her fair skin has started to tan with her recent time in the sun. She is shorter than average, and her green eyes are almost always looking at the dirt.

In contrast, Nettie's thick red hair is hastily braided into a ponytail. Nettie doesn't tan in the sun. Instead, her cheeks and hands freckle. Nettie almost never looks down, and her blue-eyed glare can raise the hair on many necks.

"Take the horses out and get them running," Ms. Wilkerson says.

"Just follow Nettie," Mrs. Dickens tells Birdie. "But don't let Nettie get ya goin' too fast. Dixie needs to run. But if ya go too fast, you'll just hurt her leg."

"Don't worry, Mrs. Dickens," Birdie replies. "I'll take it easy."

"I'll go a lil' bit slower than Taylor's fastest," Nettie adds.

"I want ya to go a lot slower than Taylor's fastest."

"Yes, ma'am," Nettie replies as she finds her stirrup and swings onto Taylor.

Birdie hesitates but then swings onto Dixie. She trots the black in a tight circle. Birdie breathes uneasily and looks uncomfortable in the saddle, her oversized pants and shirt adding to her discomfort.

"Relax, Birdie," Mrs. Dickens tells the girl. "You'll do fine."

"Follow me, Birdie," Nettie says, nice and loud. "I'll show ya where to go."

The big bay jumps to a start and exits the ranch gate in a cloud of dust.

Birdie waits for the cloud to clear and then lopes easily behind.

Nettie lets Taylor run as fast as he wants on the flat road just outside the ranch. Taylor can really run, but Nettie is disappointed that she can't get that last little burst of speed out of him like she can on Dixie.

Nettie veers off the road and turns out of the valley onto a small side trail. She pulls Taylor to a stop and looks back down the road for Birdie.

Where is she? Nettie wonders. *I'll have my job back in no time.*

Nettie waits for about a minute before Birdie and Dixie come up the road. The new jockey reaches Nettie and pulls her horse to a stop.

"Aren't ya goin' too fast?" Birdie asks. "I'm not sure where I'm goin'."

"I think ya need to go a lil' bit faster," Nettie coaxes.

"Didn't ya lose your job for goin' too fast? I like the pace I'm goin'."

"I know they want ya to go slow," Nettie says, "but they meant for a racehorse. And slow for a racehorse is still pretty fast."

"I think I'll keep the slower pace," Birdie says. "I'm quite capable of followin' instructions."

"Fine by me," Nettie says, with a toss of her braid. "Goin' slow will just get me back on my racehorse sooner."

"Nothin' would make me happier than losin' my job," Birdie says matter of factly. "I don't really like ridin' anyway."

Nettie is speechless. She shakes her head and digs her heels into Taylor. The big bay jumps back into action. They gradually gallop out of the valley and follow a trail across a wide-open flat.

Nettie looks back and sees Birdie in the distance. Nettie slows Taylor to match Dixie's pace. Nettie is irritated, but she knows her only job is to show Birdie the trail. So Nettie slows her horse, and Birdie catches up.

Nettie doesn't feel like talking, so she stays just ahead of Birdie and Dixie.

Down valleys and along creeks the two riders and two horses run. Through trees and around rocky ledges they run. The sun rises and heats up the valley as the jockey and groom exercise their horses.

As Nettie approaches the Wilkerson Ranch, she slows even more and lets Birdie and the black colt catch up. The two girls ride their horses through the wooden gate and into the yard. In a cloud of dust, Nettie pulls up her big bay. Just behind Nettie, Birdie ambles into the ranch yard under the watchful eyes of Ms. Wilkerson and Mrs. Dickens.

The two women walk quickly to Birdie and Dixie.

Boy, oh, boy. Birdie is really gonna get it, Nettie thinks. *Dixie isn't even breathin' hard and has barely broken a sweat.* Nettie pulls closer so she can hear the chastising.

Birdie dismounts, and Mrs. Dickens runs her hand up and down the little black's front left leg.

"There's no heat here," Mrs. Dickens says. "Did she limp on it at all?"

"She was a lil' stiff on it first thing," Birdie says, betraying that she knows more about horses than she lets on. "But I kept it slow at the start and then went a lil' faster when she loosened up."

"Good, Birdie, good," Ms. Wilkerson says. "You rode her just right."

Nettie's ears burn. *Just right!* she fumes. *Birdie was goin' way too slow!*

"I agree," Mrs. Dickens says as she strokes the little colt. "She feels good and looks really good too."

"Well done, Birdie," Ms. Wilkerson says. "We will engage the same plan tomorrow."

"What!" Nettie exclaims. "Ya want Birdie to ride Dixie tomorrow?"

"Yes, Nettie," Ms. Wilkerson replies. "Our arrangement worked out perfectly today. I am skeptical that your role in the process is really necessary."

Nettie stares at Ms. Wilkerson in horror. Instead of being angry at Birdie's slow pace, she is now questioning Nettie's value.

When Nettie first came to work for Ms. Wilkerson, she was a perfect jockey. Ms. Wilkerson wanted a jockey to ride her horses fast, and that is exactly what Nettie did.

Recently, though, Ms. Wilkerson and Mrs. Dickens have wanted Nettie to become a more refined jockey. They are trying to teach her to change her mount's pace and switch between pushing and resting her horse.

These techniques would make Nettie a better jockey. But Nettie is only interested in riding fast. And in the minds of owner and trainer, a jockey who isn't improving is expendable.

"Nettie is very important," Birdie says. "I wouldn't know where to go without her."

"The route is unimportant," Ms. Wilkerson blurts out as though Nettie isn't within earshot. "Nettie's services are no longer required."

"If Nettie isn't leadin' me, then I won't ride," Birdie says.

"Then I will fire you," Ms. Wilkerson says with a raised eyebrow.

"That's fine by me," Birdie says as she throws her hands up. "I didn't want this job. Let Nettie ride your horse."

"Now wait," Ms. Wilkerson says as she takes a step back. "Let us not be hasty. If we continue with the current arrangement, would everyone be happy?"

Birdie looks at Nettie, and Nettie replies, "I don't know that anybody is really happy, includin' ya, Ms. Wilkerson. But I think we can make it work."

"It's okay by me," Birdie says.

"Then it is settled," Ms. Wilkerson says. "Walk your horses out and be here tomorrow at first light."

"Yes, ma'am," Birdie and Nettie groan at the same time.

THE TWO GIRLS SIT on the front porch of the Three Creek Store, across from a large barn that serves as a dance hall when it's empty in the spring. Both suck on cinnamon sticks.

The sun is high, and the heat of the day is rolling in. The girls hide from the heat in the shade of the front porch.

"So, why'd ya do it?" Nettie asks.

Birdie looks puzzled. "Whattaya mean?"

"Why'd ya stand up for me?"

"I don't know," Birdie says with a shrug. "I don't know my way around. I need a guide."

"I'm not buyin' it," Nettie says. "There's no set route, and ya have the pace down."

Birdie stares at her toes.

"I don't really need to ride horses," she says.

Nettie gasps.

"I don't need a job," Birdie continues. "I don't need the money. The one thing I'm missin' is a friend."

"So that's why ya insisted on followin' me?" Nettie asks.

"That's right," Birdie replies. "I couldn't care less 'bout the job or ridin' or any of that — unless I get to do it with ya."

Nettie doesn't know what to say. She's never had a friend, much less a friend who would give up her job just to spend more time with her.

"Er, thanks," Nettie replies roughly.

Birdie sits on the porch and works the cinnamon stick around her tongue. She savors the flavor for a little bit. "You're welcome." She pauses again and then adds, "If ridin' horses is so important to ya, why do ya keep eatin' cinnamon sticks? Didn't Ms. Wilkerson tell ya not to?"

"I know what she says." Nettie smirks, tickled over talking about the evils of cinnamon sticks with a cinnamon stick in her mouth. "But I'll skip dinner if it means I get to eat my cinnamon stick."

"Don't skip dinner," Birdie says. "Just eat your meat and vegetables. That'll help offset the sugar."

"Good tip," Nettie says. "I'll give it a try."

The new friends finish their cinnamon sticks, talking and laughing and carrying on for another hour in the porch's shade. As the sun ducks behind the western ridge, they quickly say their goodbyes and walk home.

Chapter Five

ANOTHER MORNING, ANOTHER RIDE. For most people, the redundancy of riding day after day would be boring. But not for Nettie. The little black is hardly limping, so Birdie rides Dixie a bit faster today. Nettie sighs, wishing they could go even faster.

As the girls race up a small rise, they come across a boy with dirty hands and knees riding an athletic-looking gray horse. The boy is small for his age and sits comfortably in his saddle. A shovel is strapped behind him.

He pulls up on the reins, and the gray stops in Nettie's path.

"It's wild-haired Nettie," the boy says with an evil grin.

"I'm not in the mood, Otis," Nettie says with a scowl. "Ya tripped my horse!"

"I don't know what you're talkin' 'bout," Otis says.

Nettie pauses. *Maybe it wasn't Otis.* Then Nettie notices the same kind of braided rawhide rope as a makeshift belt around Otis's waist. *He's not even smart enough to cover his tracks.*

"Ya know exactly what I'm talkin' 'bout. Ya can make fun of me, but don't mess with my horse."

"Your brain must be numb," Otis says as he looks away. "I didn't tie a rope across the trail."

"I didn't mention a rope or trail!" Nettie yells. "Stop or I *will* make ya stop."

"Ya have to catch me first," Otis taunts.

Otis kicks Mercury and then pulls back on the reins. The confused horse bites his bit.

"Get out of my way!" Otis yells at Nettie. His nostrils flare, and the whites of his eyes start turning red.

"I'm not in your way," Nettie says with narrowed eyes. "If I were, ya wouldn't be able see over me."

Otis scowls as he digs his heels into the gray horse, and they race down the trail.

"Who was that?" Birdie asks. "A friend of yours?"

Otis and Nettie should be friends. They have so much in common. They are the same age. They are jockeys, and both enjoy insulting the other. Both even exhibit the overconfidence of people who routinely control seemingly out-of-control, powerful animals. And they are competitive, which might be the source of their friction.

They have been racing each other for years, and their competitiveness has spilled into a strong dislike for each other.

"Otis is not a friend," Nettie spits. "Otis is the worst of the booger-eatin' boys who live around here. And, believe me, all of 'em are booger eaters."

"That's really gross," Birdie says. "All the boys eat their boogers?"

"Well, not actually," Nettie replies. "But ya get the idea. They are really gross and annoyin'."

"What's Otis doin' out here?" Birdie asks.

"He's probably doin' the same thing we are, exercisin' his horse before the race," Nettie says and then looks thoughtful. *But he's usually not so dirty.*

"Is his horse any good?" Birdie asks.

"Yeah. Mercury is the horse to beat," Nettie says. "They won last year."

"Can we beat him?" Birdie asks.

"Dixie is faster," Nettie says confidently. "But Otis and Mercury are bullies. Ya can't just outrun them; ya have to outrace them."

"How?"

"It's not always the fastest horse that wins," Nettie says. "Mercury will speed out to a lead and then spend the rest of the race barin' his teeth, intimidatin' any horse that threatens to pass. And Otis is just as bad. I've seen him smack a trailin' horse in the face to slow him down. He even set up a trip rope for Dixie a few days ago."

"He tripped her!" Birdie gasps. "So they're not the fastest, just the meanest?"

"That's right. That's why she's been limpin'," Nettie replies. "So to win, we need to teach Dixie to pass a bully."

"How?" Birdie asks.

"I don't know."

Nettie pulls Taylor back onto the trail and jumps to a gallop. Birdie and the little black dutifully follow.

About 200 yards away, Nettie spies a tree branch across the trail, and suddenly Otis's shovel and dirty hands and knees come to mind.

Nettie pulls Taylor to a stop and dismounts. She walks just beyond the branch and sees a freshly dug hole poorly covered with sagebrush.

Otis Gregerson, Nettie thinks, seeing red. *That horse's butt is gonna get it! I'm gonna make him eat horse apples this time!*

"How'd that hole get there?" Birdie asks, pulling Dixie to a stop.

"Stinkin' Otis is tryin' to keep Dixie from racin'!" Nettie says as she angrily throws the branch and brush aside before kicking enough dirt into the hole to make the trail safe again.

"That's awful!" Birdie cries. "We could have been hurt!"

"Fortunately, he isn't very good at settin' traps," Nettie says. "That lil' twerp is gettin' dangerous though."

I'm gonna get ya, Otis Gregerson, Nettie vows as she remounts and leads Birdie and Dixie down the trail. *But I'm glad to know you're worried 'bout Dixie's speed. Perhaps a test race would be just the thing.*

Nettie smiles, doing a little plotting of her own.

THE PARLOR OF Ms. Wilkerson's house is cool and dimly lit. The furniture is ornate, and portraits decorate every wall.

Mrs. Dickens and Birdie sip glasses of sun tea as the graying trainer explains the finer points of riding bareback and the superiority of spotted horses. Birdie nods, wide eyed.

Ms. Wilkerson sashays into the parlor and with great fanfare adjusts her dress and sits. The two older women begin talking about details of operating the horse ranch before speaking casually about how Dixie ran.

Nettie is afraid to touch the fancy glass. So she leaves her sun tea on the small table next to her fancy floral-print chair, which she suspects is getting dusty following her ride.

Nettie sees a small chunk of horse poop fall off her boot, so she quietly scoops it up and puts it in her pocket. "Er," she says. "I've been thinkin' 'bout the race and Mercury."

"Yes?" Ms. Wilkerson asks as she adjusts the spoon next to her tea. Ms. Wilkerson is always moving or primping or straightening.

"Well, ya know how he's a bully?" Nettie asks.

"That's how he's won every race, runnin' out to an early lead and usin' his teeth and guile to keep the other horses from passin'," Mrs. Dickens agrees.

"Well, Birdie and I were wonderin' how to get Dixie to pass a bully like that."

"That is a great question, Nettie," Ms. Wilkerson replies. "We need a strategy." Ms. Wilkerson says "we," but she looks directly at Mrs. Dickens.

Mrs. Dickens looks to the left and to the right. Mrs. Dickens' eyebrows draw down in thought.

"What 'bout a test race?" Nettie asks her.

"Yes!" Mrs. Dickens says, nearly cracking a smile. "If Dixie runs beside Mercury a couple times, she might get used to him and be less intimidated."

"How do we arrange that?" Ms. Wilkerson asks.

"Let me take care of that," Nettie replies with a wicked grin. "With my special ability of gettin' under people's skin, I think I can goad Otis into a couple secret races."

"You are quite keen at the art of irritation," Ms. Wilkerson agrees, looking a little pained as she remembers Nettie's horrid table manners and loose application of the truth when it comes to riding. "Do your best, Nettie."

"Is Dixie up to a race?" Birdie asks.

"Her leg wasn't too hot today," Mrs. Dickens says. "As long as she's warmed up, an easy race would help stretch it out."

Birdie nods.

"Well, go forth, girls," Ms. Wilkerson proclaims. "Our little arrangement seems better and better each day."

Nettie's smile fades. *The arrangement is workin'*, she realizes, *which means I won't be in the big race if I wanna keep my friend.*

WITH THE SPRING DERBY less than a week away, the Three Creek Store is especially busy. So Nettie and Birdie sit on the shaded front step of the nearby dance hall. Each is eating half a cinnamon stick, a compromise with Ms. Wilkerson's wishes that Birdie had suggested.

The tiny town is bustling with activity. Every spring, the stockgrowers have a big meeting. Cattle barons, sheep kings, and horse traders come from miles around. They bring their foremen and families, and this meeting transitions into the spring festival for the area.

After the long, boring meeting comes the good stuff— feasting, music, dancing, and games. The capstone is the horse race the afternoon of the last day. And if Nettie has anything to say about it, Dixie will be preening in the victor's circle.

As Nettie rolls the cinnamon stick in her mouth, savoring every particle, she notices three boys on the far side of the dance hall.

"There's Otis," Nettie says with a fiendish smile, standing. "Let's go talk to him."

Nettie almost skips as she starts over to Otis, her long-braided mane swaying as she walks. Birdie follows five steps behind with her arms folded and staring straight at the ground.

Otis stands in front of the other boys. He's about a head shorter than the other two and half a head shorter than Nettie.

"Hey, Otis," Nettie says as she skips to a stop.

"Sweaty Nettie," Otis replies, barely acknowledging her. "Seein' ya here just ruined my day."

"Why don't ya stand up and say that to my face?"

"I am standin', ya fool," Otis sneers with his hands on his hips.

"Oh, that's right," Nettie barks. "I forget that you're just shorter than everybody else."

Otis bristles.

"And I thought ya were a jockey," Nettie continues, shaking her head. "But it seems you're spendin' all your time settin' traps for my horse. Ya must be scared she's faster than yours."

"Don't make me laugh," Otis says in a rush. "Mercury is the fastest horse in the county — no, in the state! We can outrun your ol' nag any day."

"Well, I might be ridin' 'an ol' nag,'" Nettie says, "but Birdie can outrun ya on Dixie."

"I'll race her anytime, anyplace," Otis blurts, taking Nettie's bait.

"Nine o'clock tomorrow at the cave a mile up the creek," Nettie quickly replies.

"What?" Otis asks. He had been making a boast, not an offer.

"Ya said anytime, anyplace," Nettie taunts. "I gave ya a time and place, booger eater. You've got a race — unless you're scared."

Otis stares silently at Nettie. He's pretty sure he's been outwitted, but his pride prevents him from backing down. He glares at Nettie, and his nostrils flare in anger.

"I'll be there," Otis blares.

Nettie spins on her heels and walks away. She doesn't want to talk to Otis any more than she has to. Birdie follows Nettie, again at a distance with her arms folded, but now with a smile, clearly enjoying her friend's talent at riling the vile Otis.

"Looks like ya have a race in the mornin'," Nettie says to Birdie as the girls begin walking home.

"I don't know." Birdie gulps. "I've never been in a horse race before."

"This will be as good for ya as for Dixie," Nettie says.

"What should I do tomorrow?" Birdie asks. "How do I race?"

"We'll get the lil' black warmed up real good," Nettie says. "I'm sure Dixie is faster than Mercury, but ya don't need to win tomorrow."

"Wait, don't I wanna win?" Birdie asks.

"Not tomorrow," Nettie says. "We just need to get Dixie used to the stallion. Besides that, we don't wanna injure her."

"So I ride behind Mercury like I ride behind Taylor?" Birdie asks.

"Kind of like that," Nettie replies, "but closer. Ya need to run right next to his hip as long as ya can."

"Where will ya be?" Birdie asks.

"I'll be ridin' Taylor," Nettie says. "I will try to run on the gray's other hip, but Taylor just isn't fast enough to keep up."

"I'm not sure if I'm good enough to ride a horse that fast," Birdie says.

"You'll do fine," Nettie says. "Just keep your backside in the saddle."

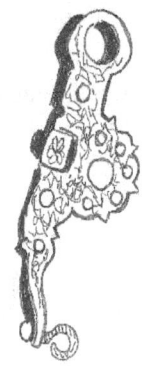

Chapter Six

NETTIE STANDS IN HER stirrups. Her knees are slightly bent to absorb the constant pounding of Taylor's hooves. Taylor is taller and stronger than Dixie, so Nettie has to work even harder to control him.

Even at the slower pace, the wind whips across Nettie's face and under the brim of her hat. The teen leans forward and urges Taylor to run faster, but he can't. Taylor eats up the trail in front of him.

The top two buttons of Nettie's shirt are unbuttoned, and her collar flaps in the wind. Her gray shirt looks almost identical to the shirt she wore yesterday. Nettie doesn't waste any more time on fashion than she needs to. In contrast, Birdie wears a light blue shirt with dark blue jeans that fit better than her outfit the day before.

Nettie and Birdie ride their horses along the same trail as the previous day. Nettie has carefully planned the morning ride so they reach the cave at nine o'clock.

We don't wanna be early, or our horses could tighten up as we wait for Otis, Nettie thinks. *But if we get there late, the lil' snake might not wait for us.*

As they round the next bend, the girls see a slight rider in a blue shirt and too-short jeans on a tall gray stallion. It's Otis, and he fidgets as he waits. Despite a recent growth spurt, he's still short. Nettie speeds up to catch him before he leaves. Birdie maintains her leisurely pace.

Nettie stops abruptly about ten yards from Otis. The dust she kicked up overtakes the two and settles on the parley.

"Mornin', Otis," Nettie says. The words are friendly, but her tone is malicious.

"Mornin', Nettie," Otis's tone is equally vile. "Let's get movin'. I have more important things to do today than look at your ugly mug."

"Ya mean ya have to meet up with your toadies and tell lies with them," Nettie goads.

"If ya were a boy, I'd punch ya," Otis threatens. Threats are Otis's favorite tool.

"If ya were a girl, I'd make fun of how short ya are," Nettie replies, knowing how best to get under Otis's skin.

As the two bicker, Birdie and Dixie ride up.

"Let's get this done with," Otis says again. "We'll race to the tree up the creek and back. How do ya wanna start?"

"You're the undisputed champion," Nettie says. "Why don't ya say 'go'?"

Otis looks Nettie up and down. He agrees he should start the race, but he's pretty sure Nettie's outsmarting him. He's just not sure how.

"Get ready," Otis says.

Birdie looks unprepared but pulls the black colt in line with the other two horses.

"Get set," Otis says.

Birdie flashes an anxious look at Nettie.

"Just do your best to keep up," Nettie whispers.

Birdie takes a deep breath.

"Go!"

Otis and Nettie spur their horses into a gallop. Birdie follows a beat behind.

Nettie pushes Taylor to run at a pace he can't sustain. Her strategy is to get Otis to race Mercury at a pace he can't maintain either. Taylor edges his nose out to a lead, but Otis and Mercury keep up.

Birdie, meanwhile, keeps Dixie right behind the gray.

Mercury angrily pins his ears back and bares his teeth at Taylor. But Taylor is an old horse and isn't intimidated. However, his age also means he will slow down as the race proceeds.

The three pairs streak to the tree at the edge of the flat, which is the halfway point, and they jockey for the best position as they run around it.

Nettie nudges Taylor closer to Mercury. She positions herself so she will have the inside route around the tree with Birdie on the outside.

Otis can see Nettie pushing him out, so he swings the reins and slaps the gray stallion on the rump. He pulls slightly ahead, but not far enough to displace Nettie's inside track.

He swings the reins and slaps the gray again. Mercury bares his teeth and snaps at Taylor. But Taylor ignores him. Meanwhile, Birdie and Dixie race comfortably at the stallion's hip.

As the three round the tree, the gray horse noses out to a lead. Despite Nettie's urging, Taylor slows and drops a full length behind Mercury. To avoid injury to her horse, Nettie concedes and pulls Taylor back to a steady lope.

But Birdie stays right on Mercury's hip, keeping the reins tight to avoid passing him. Mercury eases up slightly, and Birdie slows Dixie to match the pace. The closeness annoys the gray beast, who angrily glares at the smaller horse and snaps his teeth at her.

Dixie slows down, but Birdie kicks her back into place at the stallion's hip. Mercury pins his ears back and snaps again. The colt hesitates, but Birdie kicks her back to speed before she loses any ground.

The little black's persistence angers Mercury, and he snaps at Dixie again. Birdie digs her heels into Dixie's ribs, and the small horse darts past Mercury.

Otis urges the stallion to go faster, but the stallion is running as fast as he can. Birdie, remembering Nettie's instruction, pulls back on her reins and slows Dixie, tucking her neatly behind the stallion's right hip.

The gray horse is angrier than ever. He pins his ears back again and snaps at the colt. Dixie is getting used to the stallion's ways, so she runs comfortably at his hip.

Otis and Mercury race across the finish line first. Birdie and Dixie are a very close second, and Nettie and Taylor are a distant third.

Despite losing the race, Nettie smiles from ear to ear.

"Great race, Birdie!" Nettie congratulates.

"Great race?" Otis questions. "What's so great 'bout a race ya lose?"

"She could've won."

"Whattaya mean?" Otis asks.

"Birdie raced past Mercury but held Dixie back at the end," Nettie says. "If she let her run, she would've won easily."

"Nuh uh," Otis disagrees loudly, but Nettie can see in his eyes that he knows she's right.

"A winner is a winner," Otis replies defensively.

"I know," Nettie says. "Ya won. I'm just sayin' Birdie let ya win."

"That's a load of horse crap!" Otis can't come up with a better comeback.

"I don't know that I let the stallion win," Birdie says as she looks up and makes eye contact with Otis. The youth nods his head and smiles. "But I did slow down at the end."

Otis stops nodding. Every instinct in his body screams that Nettie is setting a trap for him, but his pride forces him to speak.

"I can beat ya or anybody else — any day, any time," Otis blurts.

"Tomorrow," Nettie quickly replies, "same time and same place."

Standing in the trap, Otis is now certain Nettie has set a trap for him. But he has no idea what she is scheming.

"I'll be here," Otis yells after Nettie and Birdie, who are already heading down the trail.

Otis angrily shakes his head. Only Nettie McCorkle could make him feel like he lost a race he actually won. Befuddled, Otis turns Mercury in the opposite direction and jogs down the trail.

BACK AT THE McCORKLE homestead, it's as chaotic as ever. Nettie's mother untangles a ball of yarn while rocking in a chair on the front porch. Nine-year-old Melly practices playing the spoons. When done correctly, the spoons are a catchy and musical art of percussion. As performed by Melly, though, it's just noise.

Five-year-old Bucket is on his hands and knees in the front yard playing with the family dog. The little boy snaps his teeth at the timid cow dog, which growls and snaps back. Nettie rolls her eyes. It's just like her brother to act like a rabid dog.

Nettie's father sits on the front porch, working on something in his hands.

"Whatcha doin', Daddy?" Nettie asks as she walks over and sits on a nearby bench.

"I dropped my reins when I was ridin' Clyde this mornin', and he stepped on 'em."

Nettie nods, picturing the giant draft horse clumsily stepping on his rein, throwing his head in the air, and tightening the rein until it snapped with a crack.

"How was your day?" Mr. McCorkle asks without looking up from his work.

"We had a great workout with Dixie this mornin'," Nettie says. "I suckered Otis into a race, and we were able to pretty much beat that gray stallion he rides."

"Mercury is fast and mean," Mr. McCorkle says. "Ya should be proud to beat him."

"I'm not sure I'm all that happy 'bout it," Nettie says, spilling the honest truth.

"Why?"

"Well, I wasn't ridin' Dixie," Nettie says. "Birdie was. I had Taylor race the stallion out to a pace he couldn't keep so Birdie and Dixie could win."

"I still don't see the problem," Mr. McCorkle replies.

"Well, I wanna be the jockey," Nettie whines. "But this is workin' so well that I doubt Ms. Wilkerson will change anythin'."

"You're probably right. It would be foolish to change somethin' that's workin'. Let me tell ya a lil' secret. It's amazin' what can be accomplished when it doesn't matter who gets the glory."

"But I want the credit."

"That might be the only problem then." Mr. McCorkle pauses to let his words sink in. "Ya have the expertise to set a pace the stallion can't maintain, right?"

"That's right," Nettie replies.

"And Birdie knows only enough to ride Dixie just as ya instruct?"

"Yes."

"And if ya switched, would it still work?"

Nettie pauses and scrunches her face. She knows the answer, but she doesn't want to voice the painful truth. "It wouldn't work if we switched," she finally replies.

"Do ya think the lil' colt could beat the stallion without the fast pace at the start? Could ya beat the stallion alone?"

"I doubt it." Nettie sighs. "But when Dixie wins, all the glory will go to the jockey. I'm doin' all the work and comin' up with the plan, and Birdie is gonna get all the credit."

"It's amazin' what can be accomplished when it doesn't matter who gets the glory," Mr. McCorkle says again.

It's annoyin' when a parent repeats himself, Nettie thinks. She smiles at her witty comeback. Her father nods happily, misinterpreting the smile as getting through to his stubborn daughter.

"So you're sayin' that I should do the best I can at my job and be happy if Birdie wins," Nettie says.

"It's your choice," Mr. McCorkle says. "But that's what I would do."

Chapter Seven

THE NEXT MORNING IS overcast. Birdie and Nettie prepare their horses for exercise as Ms. Wilkerson and Mrs. Dickens walk out of the white-pillared Victorian-style ranch house through the yard and past a storage shed and lean-to blacksmith shed before reaching the girls.

Ms. Wilkerson wears a stiff dark blue dress with a blue shawl and a lacey white collar, which clinches tightly to her neck. *I wonder if Ms. Wilkerson walks so straight and proper just to keep from chokin',* Nettie considers.

Mrs. Dickens looks more comfortable in pants, riding boots, and her customary beaded vest. A poncho covers her shoulders for warmth.

"We are two days out," Ms. Wilkerson admonishes the girls. "It is critical to get it right now."

"Ride her easy," Mrs. Dickens says slowly, enunciating every word. "Except when ya run against the stallion. Keep Dixie right on his hip, but let's finish at the same time. We'll save the win for the real race."

"Ms. Wilkerson?" Nettie says.

"Yes, Nettie, what is it?"

"I had an idea as we were ridin' yesterday," Nettie replies. "I was able to set a fast pace with Taylor at the start of the race. It was too fast for Taylor to keep up."

"Go on," Ms. Wilkerson says.

"Well, it was too fast for Mercury too," Nettie says. "So I was wonderin' if ya could enter me and Taylor in the race. We could get out to a fast start and stretch out the stallion so he doesn't have the strength to close out the race."

"That just might work," Mrs. Dickens says. She is excited about the idea, but, as always, she does a masterful job at hiding her emotion. "Teamin' up on the gray can set the pace in our favor."

"I like the idea too," Birdie says. "I'm not very experienced as a jockey. I have trouble settin' the pace."

"It would cost me an extra entry fee," Ms. Wilkerson says. "Is it our only chance to win?"

"I'm not sure if it's our only chance, but I'd say it's our best chance," Nettie replies.

"I agree," Mrs. Dickens says. "With Nettie as pacesetter, our lil' black will have a leg up on that mean, ol' gray stallion."

"Well, then, go test the strategy again, girls," Ms. Wilkerson says. "I will see if I can muster together a second entry fee."

Nettie giggles with excitement at the prospect of racing in the derby, even if it is riding Taylor.

WITH THE CHILLY MORNING, the girls take a little bit longer warming up their horses, taking a shorter route to meet Otis. They dart around sagebrush and bounce over rocks. As the sun creeps higher, the horses' muscles warm. At the top of a bluff overlooking the flat where they raced yesterday, Nettie and Birdie stop to survey the course.

Otis isn't here yet. He probably wants to make us wait this time, Nettie thinks.

"So the plan is the same as yesterday?" Birdie asks.

"Yep. Everythin' is the same except this time pull up even with the stallion as ya cross the finish line," Nettie says.

"Aren't ya worried Otis will figure out our plan?" Birdie asks.

"Not really. Otis wasn't smart enough to figure out we were usin' his horse for practice yesterday. And here he comes again," Nettie replies, nodding toward the slender teen riding up in the distance.

"Do ya think he's set some sort of a trap again, like the rope or hole?" Birdie asks.

"I don't know," Nettie replies. "But if he did somethin', we'll figure it out. Otis is a trickster, but he's not very sneaky. Once when we were lil', Otis dipped my braid in an ink bottle."

"Ya knew it was him?" Birdie asks as the girls walk their horses over to the tree they use for the start and finish line.

"He was the only one with ink on his fingers."

"So what did ya do?"

"I dropped part of an ant pile down his pants," Nettie says, grinning hugely. "He had ants in his pants for the rest of the day."

Nettie and Birdie burst into laughter as Otis gallops up.

"You're late, Otis," Nettie says.

"It's only fair," Otis replies, eyeing the girls warily. "Ya were late yesterday."

"And we started the race right when we got here, so get on the line."

"Now wait," Otis exclaims. "Give my horse a chance to catch his breath."

"Fine," Nettie says since they don't want to win the race today, "but that means I get to start the race."

"Okay by me," Otis says, pretending to be confident. Secretly, though, he's certain Nettie is scheming — and that he is two or three moves behind her.

"I'm ready," Otis says as he pulls Mercury on the line. Otis is done trying to outsmart Nettie, so he moves straight to action.

"Are ya ready, Birdie?" Nettie asks.

Birdie nods.

Otis squirms, increasingly annoyed about being stuck between two gossipy, giggly girls.

"On your mark," Nettie hesitates. "Get set," she hesitates for a count longer. "Go!"

In a flurry, the three horses jump to a start. Because Nettie started the race, she queues Taylor into action a half count before the other two. So Nettie and Taylor take the early lead. Otis and Mercury are a head behind, and Birdie rides Dixie comfortably beside the gray's right hip.

Taylor pulls away, but the stallion keeps him close. Mercury pins his ears back and bares his teeth in anger. Taylor is unfazed. The stallion decides to outrun the old horse instead.

Mercury surges forward, but Nettie urges Taylor to keep the lead. Halfway through the first leg, Taylor and Mercury run neck and neck. Nettie digs her heels into Taylor's ribs to urge more speed. But the big bay fades again, and the stallion pulls into the lead.

Birdie and Dixie are still tucked to the right of Mercury's hip, just as planned. The three pairs whip around the turnaround tree with the stallion leading, the little black in second, and Taylor bringing up the rear.

As they race back the way they'd come, Birdie slacks the reins until Dixie and Mercury are nose and nose. Birdie pulls back on the reins to avoid passing, faithfully executing the plan.

The gray snaps his teeth at the colt, but Dixie is getting used to the stallion's shenanigans. Mercury pins his ears back and snaps unsuccessful again.

Taking in his horse's second failed attempt at bullying, Otis decides to try his own — and he pulls his reins hard to the right. The big stallion bolts into the side of the smaller black horse, bouncing Dixie to the right. She stumbles on a rock and launches Birdie from the saddle.

Nettie watches in horror as Birdie flies through the air and flops hard on the ground. Otis races away toward the finish line. Nettie stops Taylor and hastily dismounts. Birdie lies motionless before slowly sitting up and making a loud wheezing sound.

"Lie back down," Nettie says, taking control. "You've had the wind knocked out of you."

Birdie groans and can't seem to inhale. Her hair is disheveled, and she is covered in dirt.

"Just relax your stomach," Nettie says as she presses on Birdie's middle. Birdie inhales deeply and her groan softens. She takes another deep breath.

"It hurts!" Birdie finally cries out. "It really hurts."

"What hurts?" Nettie asks.

"My arm!" Birdie cries out again. "I can't move my arm, and it hurts!"

Nettie immediately guesses the problem. She unties her scarf and refolds it into a triangle. Nettie places Birdie's hurt arm in the folded black-and-white plaid scarf and then ties the ends around the back of Birdie's neck to fashion a makeshift sling.

Birdie's eyes glisten, and she bleeds from scrapes on her cheek. Nettie knows tears will flow when the excitement and fear wear off.

"It hurts," Birdie cries. "Is it broken?"

"I don't know. We need a doctor."

"It all happened so fast," Birdie whines with pain. "I'm not even sure what happened."

"Ya did everythin' ya were supposed to," Nettie reassures, standing. "Ya didn't do anythin' wrong."

"Then how did I end up on the ground?"

"The stallion tried to bully Dixie, but it didn't work," Nettie replies as she checks on the colt. She runs her hand up and down the horse's sore leg, which isn't hot. Nettie sighs with relief. "So Otis pulled Mercury into Dixie to knock her off balance. When she stumbled, ya tumbled over."

Nettie circles Dixie, watching her leg. The little black horse has no noticeable limp.

"Isn't that against the rules?" Birdie asks.

"It's a horse race," Nettie says. "There's only one rule: The first horse to cross the finish line wins." Nettie helps Birdie to stand and then adjusts Birdie's scarf sling. "I've seen fistfights durin' a race."

"Really? Fistfights?" Birdie says, still a bit dazed.

"And I heard 'bout a race in Colorado where a jockey pulled a gun and shot another jockey," Nettie says, her eyes bulging.

"Is that true?" Birdie asks.

"I don't know. I doubt it," Nettie mutters, walking over to the old bay horse. "But it makes a great story."

"What 'bout my arm?"

"I'll help ya get on Taylor, and I'll ride Dixie," Nettie says. "Let's go find Doc Asdale. He'll know what to do."

A victorious Otis makes his way back to the girls.

"Is everybody all right?" Otis sneers with a half smile. "I was so far ahead in the race I didn't see what happened."

"Ya know exactly what happened!" Nettie yells at Otis. Her fists are clenched, and Otis can see rage in her eyes.

Otis realizes he doesn't want to be in the same place as a furious Nettie, so he tugs on the left rein, and horse and rider gallop away.

"Don't let your guard down, ya steamin' pile of horse apples!" Nettie threatens.

Chapter Eight

THE STORE'S MORNING CUSTOMERS are just beginning to arrive. With the stockgrowers meeting so soon, a lot of people are in the area who wouldn't normally be. Most are still down at the tiny hotel or one of the boarding houses that dot the small community.

"Has anybody seen Doc Asdale?" Nettie asks loudly as she approaches the store. "I heard he was in town for the meetin'."

Mr. Reed steps onto the porch. "You're lookin' for Doc Asdale?"

"My friend, Birdie, fell off her horse," Nettie says. "Her arm's hurt real bad, and I think it's broke."

"I'll go get him," Mr. Reed says with concern as he takes in the girls' disheveled appearances and Birdie's tear-streaked face. "The hotel is full, so Doc is stayin' in the store's livin' quarters."

Mr. Reed ducks back into the store and reemerges with the good doctor.

In truth, Doc Asdale isn't actually a doctor. He's the area brand inspector. His job is to inspect various brands on cattle and horses to make sure no one is stealing livestock. He also settles ownership disputes between livestock owners.

So why is he known as "Doc"? His real name is Joseph, but most folks don't know that. In Pennsylvania a long while back, Doc Asdale went to college to become a doctor. For the first two years, he excelled. The books and lectures he studied gave him the tools to diagnose and treat any ailment from angina to zygomycosis.

In his third year of college, Doc Asdale's program changed. They spent less time in the classroom and more time in the hospital. Doc Asdale did fine with coughs, colds, and runny noses. He effectively treated any flu, measles, or other infectious diseases. Setting broken bones was no problem either.

But at the sight of blood, Doc Asdale passed out. It is very difficult — no, impossible — to finish medical school if you can't stand the sight of blood.

So Doc Asdale moved West. He picked up any work he could and eventually settled into being the area's brand inspector.

Now living in a community two days' ride from the nearest doctor, his skills as a physician are appreciated. And everyone knows that as long as you're not bleeding, Doc Asdale can fix what ails you.

"It's definitely broken," Doc says as he inspects Birdie's arm.

"Can ya fix it?" Birdie asks.

"It's not displaced," Doc Asdale says. "So I can splint it, and it will be as good as new in 'bout two months."

"But Birdie has to race Saturday!" Nettie protests.

"I wouldn't if I were her," Doc Asdale says as he pulls out two slats of wood. "If she falls again, she could break it clean through. Then her arm would never work right again."

"So no ridin'?" Birdie asks hesitantly with a nervous look at Nettie.

"No ridin'," Doc Asdale affirms. He takes a cord of cloth and rips it into three-inch-wide, three-foot-long strips. He holds the wood in place and wraps the bandages around the wood to form a splint.

"Chew on willow bark if the pain gets too bad," Doc Asdale orders. "It tastes terrible, but most medicines do."

As Doc Asdale finishes, he looks directly at Nettie. "And now for you, Nettie."

"But there's nothin' wrong with me, Doc," Nettie says, her head recoiling in surprise.

"Not yet, but I've been meanin' to talk to ya 'bout your weight," he says delicately.

"Not ya too!" Nettie protests. "I'm doin' everythin' I can to be light enough to race."

"That's the problem, Nettie," Doc says, his eyes kind. "Ya are too thin for a girl your height and age. I'm not talkin' 'bout racin'. I'm talkin' 'bout your health — your future."

"Whattaya mean, Doc?"

"I've seen too many jockeys do strange and often unhealthy things to keep their weights down. Most attempts don't work, and many jockeys end up with serious health problems."

"But I've got to be a jockey," Nettie replies as she stares at the floor. "Even if that means skippin' a meal or two."

"That's the same thing your father said twenty years ago when he was a jockey."

"He got too heavy and had to stop racin'," Nettie says sadly.

"It was more than that," Doc Asdale replies. "He hit a growth spurt the winter of his fourteenth birthday. When the spring racin' season started, he was four inches taller and 'bout twenty-five pounds heavier. He did everythin' he could to lose that weight all spring long.

"He eventually started eatin' meals and then forcin' himself to throw 'em back up. After 'bout two weeks, everythin' he ate would come back up. He couldn't keep food down even when he wanted to."

Doc places a hand on Nettie's shoulder to draw her eyes from the ground to his.

"That's how I ended up treatin' him," Doc continues. "He passed out one day while he was cleanin' stalls. He stayed with me for a week. His kidneys and stomach weren't functionin' properly. I was able to get him up and goin' again, but he really wasn't himself for a few months afterward."

"But, Doc, racin' horses is my life. It's the only thing I'm good at!" Nettie cries in panic, eyes wide. "I have to race!"

"Well, as an athlete, ya should eat like one," Doc says firmly despite his kind eyes. "That means lots of meat and lots of fruits and vegetables. Sugar, on the other hand, causes water retention and isn't good fuel for athletes. Regardless, to be healthy, ya need to gain 'bout ten pounds."

"But if I gain ten pounds, I can't race anymore!" Nettie's voice quavers. "And what if I grow taller?"

"Ya probably will," Doc Asdale says matter-of-factly. "And when ya grow taller, you'll need to gain even more weight to be healthy. People come in all sizes, Nettie. And healthy comes in all shapes. But you're underweight right now. The cruel reality is ya are just too tall to continue to be a jockey."

Nettie's face turns ghostly white.

"Then there's no way I can be a jockey," Nettie chokes, barely able to speak the cold truth. A tear escapes from the corner of her eye.

"I'm afraid that's right," Doc Asdale consoles. "If ya can't be competitive ten to twenty pounds heavier, then I would say your racin' days are over."

Nettie stares speechless into the distance. Doc Asdale's words were calm and direct but more hurtful than any Nettie had heard about her weight before.

Birdie sits silently having watched Nettie grow more and more pale as the conversation went on.

"Er, thanks, Doc," Birdie says when she realizes Nettie is incapable of talking. "How can we pay you?"

"I don't accept payments since I'm really a brand inspector," he says with a quick smile. But win the race tomorrow, Nettie. I've bet money on Dixie."

"Nettie will do her best," Birdie replies.

She stands and uses her good arm to grab a dazed Nettie by the hand. The two reach the horses, collect their reins, and head off on foot toward the Wilkerson Ranch — one girl newly bandaged and one with a newly broken heart.

AT THE WILKERSON RANCH, Mrs. Dickens prepares to mount a saddle-less horse. Ms. Wilkerson paces rapidly nearby.

"There you are!" Ms. Wilkerson nearly shouts, sashaying swiftly to the girls. "Mrs. Dickens was just about to go looking for you."

The ranch owner's hawk-like eyes narrow as she takes in the ragged girls. "It appears you had trouble. Tell me every detail."

Nettie's eyes remain vacant and her lips stay silent.

"Um," Birdie begins, looking between her friend and Ms. Wilkerson. "We went to the store so I could see Doc Asdale."

Ms. Wilkerson quickly sizes up Birdie's injury as Mrs. Dickens glides over. "What happened?"

"It was all my fault," Birdie begins.

"I doubt that," Ms. Wilkerson interrupts. She stands straight and tall and her eyes glare at Birdie. "Speak up and speak strong, Birdie."

"Well, we were runnin' next to the gray stallion," Birdie says a little louder and stronger than before. "When Dixie wouldn't back down, Otis pulled Mercury into her. She stumbled, and I fell and broke my arm."

With thought of the odious Otis, Nettie's eyes fill will rage, snapping her out of her daze.

"Oh, Birdie," Ms. Wilkerson says. "If anyone is to blame, I am. What was I thinking sending an inexperienced rider against a bully and a brute?"

"Otis Gregerson," Nettie spits his name like a curse word, "is the one to blame."

"True," Ms. Wilkerson concedes with a nod. "Nettie, I trust you will make it known to this Otis boy, in your own charming way, that his actions are unacceptable."

"I'm prepared to use both my charms," Nettie says through gritted teeth as she shakes her fists.

Nettie is having a really bad day and, in her mind, all of her troubles are tied to Otis.

The trip rope. The hole, she seethes. *Birdie's broken arm. The talk with Doc Asdale. I will smash in his smug face,* she vows.

"Now, Nettie, I do not want you to injure him," Ms. Wilkerson warns. "Just make it clear that his and his horse's actions are unacceptable."

Mrs. Dickens nods in agreement and then asks, "And what of the race?"

"Let Nettie ride," Birdie blurts out, throwing a quick glance at her friend. "She should've been your jockey all along, and Doc says I can't risk ridin' with my arm like this."

"There is a problem with that plan," Ms. Wilkerson says, rubbing her forehead. "While you two were out exercising the horses, I entered Taylor and Nettie in the race. I cannot withdraw them without losing my entry fee."

"They'll let ya switch riders, won't they?" Mrs. Dickens asks as she casually leans against a hitching post.

"I believe so," Ms. Wilkerson replies.

"Then I'll ride Taylor," Mrs. Dickens says, "and Nettie'll ride Dixie."

"Are you able?" Ms. Wilkerson asks with a raised eyebrow.

"I'm not as light as I used to be," Mrs. Dickens says with an eye roll. "But I can ride Taylor out to enough of a lead to wear down the stallion."

"And I can get Dixie past Mercury down the stretch," Nettie replies confidently, her anger ebbing with the prospect of riding the colt again. "I'm sure we can win."

"It is settled then," Ms. Wilkerson says. "We will let the horses rest tomorrow and ride them hard and fast Saturday."

THE DAY HAS BEEN long and taxing. Neither girl knows what to say to her parents about their adventures, so Nettie and Birdie head to the store instead of going home.

Birdie wants to think up a reassuring story so her parents won't ban her from the Wilkerson Ranch. Even though Birdie has no interest in being a jockey, she likes spending time with Nettie, and she admires the two strong women who run the ranch.

As they settle onto the porch, Nettie sees Otis and two other boys round the corner.

"Wait here, Birdie," Nettie says as she jumps to her feet. "I'll be right back."

The skip in Nettie step is somehow ominous, and she clenches her right fist tightly.

"Hey, Nettie," Otis says, grinning smugly. "I lost ya today when—"

WHAAAACK!

A solid right fist to Otis's left eye interrupts him. Otis's head snaps back, and he covers his rapidly swelling eye with his hand.

"What was that for?" Otis shrieks.

"Don't play stupid with me!" Nettie screeches. "Ya crashed into Birdie on purpose and broke her arm!"

"She fell! I didn't break Birdie's arm," Otis spits as his eye puffs larger.

"Don't play games with me, Otis!" Nettie hisses. "Ya know exactly what happened."

"So what," Otis sneers. "You're just mad I won. If punchin' me makes ya feel better, then why don't ya just haul back and punch me aga—"

THUNNNK!

Nettie slugs Otis right in the nose. Blood gushes everywhere, and tears flow from his eyes.

"Ya hit me again!" Otis screams.

"Ya told me to, ya idiot," Nettie replies. "I just accepted your invitation. And you're right. It does make me feel better."

Nettie spins on her heels, walks back to the porch, and grab's a giggling Birdie's hand. "Let's go. I don't think we wanna be around when he gets his wits 'bout him."

"Ya really got him good," Birdie says with a cheek-to-cheek smile as the two head down the road, leaving Otis writhing in pain as his toadies gather around him uselessly.

"He broke your arm, Birdie, and that's not okay," Nettie says. "A witty comment just won't get his attention like a sock in the eyes does."

"Whatever the reason, it was awesome," Birdie says, still beaming.

Chapter Nine

THE AIR IS BRISK but not cold. The big meeting has come and gone, and most everyone is enjoying the festivities ahead of the afternoon's big race. The two girls wear light jackets with their riding clothes. Birdie's broken arm is splinted, but she otherwise looks like a groom at a racing stable. The two girls warm up Taylor and Dixie.

Mrs. Dickens and Ms. Wilkerson walk over. Mrs. Dickens is wearing riding clothes that are a little too tight.

"Not a word 'bout my clothes bein' tight," Mrs. Dickens says indignantly.

"I wasn't gonna say anythin'," Nettie replies, keeping Dixie moving.

"It's been seventeen years and two children since I raced as a jockey," Mrs. Dickens bristles. "I'd like to see if your ridin' clothes still fit after all that."

"I remember ya tellin' me a lil' 'bout growin' up ridin'," Birdie says as she stretches out Taylor.

"Yes, I am part of the YehanDeka Tribe," Mrs. Dickens replies. "We would gather with the other Shoshone, and there was always a horse race, kind of like here.

"One day, my father acquired a horse in a trade, and he was the fastest horse I've ever seen — a lil' black horse with a dappled gray rump," she says, nearly smiling. "He was quick, and I could ride him faster than any of my brothers. For three seasons in a row, I won the horse race at the rendezvous. But then I got married and had a baby. I got too heavy. And we all know that—"

"Light jockeys win races," she and the girls say in unison.

Nettie hangs her head. "That's why this is my last race," she says with a sniff. "Doc Asdale says I'm puttin' my health at risk by stayin' at this weight. I can either be healthy or a jockey. But I can't be both."

"This is probably my last race too — as an owner," Ms. Wilkerson replies.

Nettie's eyes bulge and her jaw drops.

"Raising racehorses takes a considerable sum of money, and the ranch isn't as profitable as it used to be," Ms. Wilkerson continues. "We just don't have enough money for breeding, feeding, and training racehorses, much less paying entry fees."

"But if I win, won't the prize money be enough to keep the racehorses?" Nettie asks.

"Oh, Nettie," Ms. Wilkerson says. "Winning or losing will make no difference. If you win, I will pay Mrs. Dickens' wages for the next two or three months."

Nettie tilts her head in confusion.

"Racing horses isn't really about making money," the refined ranch owner says. "It is more for my vanity. I relish raising the fastest horses around. But we lack the profits we had even a few years ago. The masses are clamoring for railroads and automobiles, not horses. And the Army no longer needs remounts."

Ms. Wilkerson's eyes seem to peer into the past.

"Time can be a vicious taskmaster, Nettie," she continues. "You are blossoming into a fine young woman, and that is closing this chapter in your life. I am afraid time's progress is changing the ranch, too, and we need to tighten our spending. No, the race today is quite simply my last chance at glory. And yours, too, it would seem."

Nettie swallows a lump in her throat and turns to check her tack one last time. *I'm gonna win for the both of us, Ms. Wilkerson*, she thinks, holding back tears.

Nettie carefully runs her fingers over Dixie's latigoes and cinches. She feels the leather, which is properly folded over the D-rings. Nettie checks the reins and headstall for any weak spots. She shines up the silver snaffle bit that will go into Dixie's mouth. The work settles her.

Ms. Wilkerson pulls out four matching silk scarves. The scarves are plaid with crisscrossing red, black, and green lines.

"With this being our last horse race, we should go out in style," Ms. Wilkerson says, handing scarves to Mrs. Dickens and Nettie. "We should have real racing silks on our saddle blankets and around our necks."

Nettie gently fingers the soft, surprisingly strong fabric. She has never touched silk before. The young jockey places the smooth silk against her cheek and pets it like a Persian house cat.

"It's too pretty to wear," Nettie exclaims.

"Nonsense," Ms. Wilkerson says. "Place it over your normal saddle blanket and under your saddle. Wear the smaller one loosely around your neck."

Nettie hastily spins the scarf around her neck and ties it into place with a square cavalry knot. Nettie pulls the scarf up to her cheek and nuzzles the silk again.

"I think the horses are stretched out," Nettie tells Mrs. Dickens. "Should we get on and warm 'em up?"

"Yes, it's time," Mrs. Dickens replies.

Nettie measures her reins, slides her foot into the stirrup, and swings onto the little black. Dixie throws her head friskily. *That's a good sign on race day*, Nettie thinks.

Mrs. Dickens strides out to where Birdie is circling Taylor. The big bay doesn't have a saddle, just the silk on his back.

"Are ya sure ya don't wanna saddle?" Birdie asks.

"I won all my races without a saddle," Mrs. Dickens responds, climbing up. "My people don't use saddles, and it's ten pounds less for Taylor to carry."

Taylor isn't wearing his customary bit and bridle either. Mrs. Dickens controls him with her feet and legs and a thin four-foot strip of braided rawhide looped below Taylor's neck that Mrs. Dickens holds in place. The older woman ties a golden eagle feather in Taylor's mane.

"The feather will give Taylor the swiftness of the eagle," she explains to the girls.

"Good luck," Ms. Wilkerson says. She looks eager to say more, but the moment passes.

THE CROWD IS HUSHED with anticipation. Five horses mill about chaotically at the starting line. Otis sits in the center atop an angry Mercury. Next to Otis is a stocky sorrel horse ridden by an older man. His horse stands quietly, patiently waiting for the race to start. Beyond the sorrel is a big brown horse ridden by a man in his early twenties. The brown horse is exceptionally cantankerous, hopping and playfully bucking. His rider seems unfazed by all the fanfare, but Nettie knows the brown isn't a threat because he is wasting all his energy at the starting line.

The final two horses, Taylor and Dixie, stand calmly to Otis's left. Mrs. Dickens looks uncomfortable atop Taylor in her too-tight riding clothes. Nettie has a smile on her face and is relaxed and ready to race. The teen spots her dad in the crowd, and they grin at each other.

As one o'clock approaches, the jockeys become more anxious. A chubby man in a black derby hat ambles to the starting line. He wears a black vest and a black bow tie. Everyone is dressed up for the festivities, but this man stands out as official. The man pulls out a polished golden pocket watch and stares intently at the ticking hands.

"Five minutes to post," the man belts out like an opera singer. "Five minutes."

As the seconds mercilessly tick off, Nettie takes a few deep breaths. The black colt begins to prance and throw her head up and down. Dixie can feel the tension of the event building.

As the time passes, the official taps the face of his pocket watch. At this obvious signal, a boy dressed in a similar black hat and black vest raises a bugle to his lips and plays the fifty-two notes of the "Call to Post." Many of the notes are out of tune and less than harmonious.

My tone-deaf sister, Melly, can make better music than this bugler, Nettie thinks.

While the tune is unrecognizable, everyone understands this as the moment when the horses line up to start the race.

The black-eyed, bruised-nose Otis walks Mercury to the start line and picks a spot near the center. He pulls the gray to a stop and stands casually. The old man on the sorrel walks to the line and stands next to Mercury.

The young man on the brown horse prances to the start line. The man pulls back on his reins, but the brown takes three steps over the line. The man pulls the brown around and lines him up again. But the brown horse walks across the starting line again. The pair will continue the dance until the starting pistol fires. The young man hopes the gun will sound in the moments that he is on the right side of the start line so he doesn't get disqualified.

Mrs. Dickens and Taylor walk up to the starting line.

Nettie guides the little black to the line next to Taylor. Nettie leaves plenty of room, though, because she wants the swift colt to run clean and not get tangled up with any other horse. The teen's nerves finally get to her, and Dixie prances and whips her head up and down. Nettie takes a deep breath and pulls back on her reins, both of which calm the pair.

"On the line," the race official says as he raises the pistol in his right hand in the air.

The crowd turns together toward the line.

"Get set," the man says.

The crowd takes a deep breath and holds it.

The young man and the brown horse can't stand still. The old man and the sorrel horse stand like a statue. The old man takes a deep breath that slightly resembles a yawn.

Mrs. Dickens stares intently into the distance, gently pulling back on her tack rein.

Otis and the gray stallion stand majestically at the starting line. Otis glares at Nettie through his good eye. The young jockey returns a mock angry look at Otis and then winks at him. Nettie is a master of unpredictability, and the wink throws off Otis for a second.

To the two teens, the race is just between them.

BANG!

And the crowd of 200 roars in exhale and jubilation, and the horses spring out as quick as striking rattlesnakes.

In a cloud of dust, the race begins.

Mrs. Dickens, anticipating the pistol, begins the race with a half-a-head lead. Otis is a head behind her, and Nettie is slightly behind both.

The firing of the pistol startled the antsy brown horse. He bucks in a tight circle. When he bucks back across the starting line, the horse stumbles and then jumps and kicks high in the air. The crowd hoots and hollers as the horse's race devolves into a bronc ride.

They collectively cheer with each jump. The jerking dislodges the young man from his seat. He stands up in the stirrups, and flops for two more jumps. As the brown horse's feet hit the ground, the young man sails through the air and lands in a heap. Unencumbered by his rider, the brown horse shows his true speed.

The riderless horse runs the fastest race — in the wrong direction. He hits the wide-open sea of sagebrush and disappears over the northern horizon before the young man can collect himself off the ground. The pair's race is over before it really starts.

In the other direction, the race is heating up. The old man and the sorrel are about three lengths behind the leaders. Taylor and Mrs. Dickens are in the lead but barely. Otis and Mercury ride next to Taylor.

The stallion glares angrily at Taylor. His ears are pinned back, and he bares his teeth like a rabid dog. Nettie and Dixie run comfortably on Mercury's hip. Nettie is relaxed and keeps steady pressure on the reins to slow the pace and save Dixie's energy.

Focus! Nettie thinks. *Just focus on our plan.*

As the three lead horses reach the halfway pole, Taylor begins to fade. The old man and the sorrel are ten lengths behind the pair, seemingly just enjoying the race instead of pushing for a comeback.

The distant crowd is enthusiastically cheering, but Nettie can hear only a jumbled rumble of hooves beating, clothes and tack flapping, and wind swooshing beneath her hat.

The three horses round the halfway pole and race back toward the start and finish line. With Mercury in the lead, Nettie and Dixie run right on his hip, and Taylor and Mrs. Dickens fall behind.

Taylor raced valiantly, but his race is over. Sensing this, Mrs. Dickens pulls on the tack rein and slows Taylor to an easy lope. Mrs. Dickens will enjoy the race from well behind the faster horses.

The gray stallion runs easily but warily looks to his right and left to bully anyone who challenges him. So far, the race has been pretty simple, but Nettie knows she must make a move if she wants to win.

For the first time in the race, Nettie slacks the reins. The little black pins her ears back, lengthens her stride, and opens up to her fastest speed. In three graceful lunges, Nettie and Dixie pull even with Otis and the gray bully.

Otis urges his horse to keep pace, which annoys the stallion even more. Mercury has no interest in outrunning the faster black horse, so he instead plans to out-bully her. The gray stallion snaps his teeth at the little black, but she ignores him.

With little effort, Nettie and Dixie pull slightly away from Mercury.

The gray beast reaches out to bite the colt. But Dixie is just far enough away that Mercury can't reach her.

Nettie glances at Otis. He looks like a squeezed pimple about to pop. He glares at Nettie, madder than his grouchy steed. Nettie watches Otis sneer and move to pull on his left rein. It's a move she's familiar with. It's the same action that forced the two horses to collide three days earlier, breaking Birdie's arm.

So she swiftly kicks Dixie in the ribs. The willing racehorse has speed in reserve. In three lightning-fast leaps, Nettie and the little black are clear of the gray stallion as Otis yanks hard on the rein to bump them. The big gray braces for impact, but there is no impact to be had.

With the unexpected move, Mercury stumbles, and Otis flies heinie-over-tea-kettle and flops to the ground with a thump and a groan as the race passes him by.

With 200 yards left in the race, Nettie and Dixie are all alone, but they don't slow. The jockey leans forward and urges the little black to go faster.

The crowd roars in excitement. Dixie pounds out the last 200 yards in a matter of seconds and the crowd goes wild.

The black colt doesn't want to stop, but Nettie pulls on the reins, and Dixie reluctantly bounces to a stop. Ms. Wilkerson walks to the finish line and grabs Dixie's reins as Nettie lowers herself to the ground. Birdie runs up right behind Ms. Wilkerson.

"Great race, Nettie!" Birdie yells above the noise of the crowd.

"That was an incredible move," Ms. Wilkerson shouts enthusiastically. "Well done, Nettie."

Mrs. Dickens crosses the finish line and sidles up to Nettie to add her congratulations.

"Great race, Nettie," Mrs. Dickens says.

Otis leads the gray stallion across the finish line. Aside from his pride and some scrapes, he is uninjured. He walks past the crowd surrounding a jubilant Nettie. Otis glares at her and then shakes his head in disbelief.

Nettie's grin grows into a full-tooth smile. To Nettie, the thrill of winning is surpassed only by the thrill of riding fast horses — and, of course, the thrill of beating Otis.

THE AFTERNOON SUN WARMS the celebratory atmosphere at the Three Creek Store. The excitement of the horse race has carried over to the picnic. The gathered mass talks, chatters, and laughs with a hundred conversations.

"I can't wait to watch your next race," Birdie tells Nettie. "I love watchin' ya win."

"Remember what Doc Asdale said? This was my last race." Nettie swallows hard to keep from crying. "You'll have to be the jockey from now on."

"I don't think so. Aren't there other horse-ridin' jobs we could do?" Birdie asks. "Couldn't we be cowboys?"

"Don't ya mean cowgirls?" Nettie replies. "My dad's horses pull hayin' equipment, and they move faster than a horse and rider followin' a herd of cows. And my dad will need help puttin' up hay."

"My dad too," Birdie replies. "But what after that?"

"We could wrangle horses," Nettie replies. "We'd get to herd other horses, and horses like to run. It's probably the fastest job short of ridin' racehorses."

"I don't care what it is as long as we get to eat cinnamon sticks," Birdie adds. The two girls take the prompt to lick their sweet and spicy treats. As they savor the tantalizing flavor, Otis walks up alone. Apparently, toadies are only loyal to winning jockeys.

"Ya better watch yourself," Otis spouts off angrily. His hair is still disheveled and a mixture of dirt and blood cakes his face and clothes. Otis is a mess.

Nettie stands up and approaches Otis cautiously like he's an injured animal.

With a maniacal look in his eyes, Otis begins. "If ya weren't a girl, I'd punch you!" Otis pauses, expecting a witty comeback.

But Nettie holds her tongue, allowing Otis to complete his rant. "It might not be today or tomorrow, but when ya least expect it, I'll be there."

Nettie's silence emboldens Otis. "Whenever ya ride, wherever ya ride, I'll be there to—"

Smmoooch! Nettie finally interrupts — with a kiss on Otis's cheek.

His eyes widen, bewildered, and he recoils a couple steps. Otis smiles a little bit and then turns green like he's eaten bad potato salad. He staggers and rubs the spot on his cheek.

Birdie, who was expecting a punch, looks like a child whose toy was just taken away.

Otis is speechless and carefully steps back three paces.

Nettie smiles and winks at him. Otis spins on his heels and runs away.

"I thought ya hated Otis," Birdie says, shocked.

"Oh, I do," Nettie replies, grinning. "But I really like to mess with him."

"I'm sure ya did that," Birdie says with a giggle. "I liked the punch better, but I think the kiss messed with his mind more."

"Ya think so?" Nettie asks, pleased. "That's what I was shootin' for."

The girls laugh and saunter off arm in arm to join the picnic.

From the author...

Nettie McCorkle and the Horse Race is fiction, but parts of the book actually happened. In early Western horse races, girls were sometimes jockeys because they were often smaller and lighter than boys their age. My great-grandmother was one such jockey, riding her uncle's quarter horses in local races.

In the early 1900s, the Wilkins Horse Ranch was the largest horse ranch west of the Mississippi River. More than ten thousand horses ranged from the Snake River in Southwestern Idaho to the Jarbidge Mountains nearly one hundred miles away. The ranch sold horses by the trainload and shipped them as far away as South Africa. And a strong woman ran the whole operation.

When her husband proved incapable of managing the family's finances, Laura Wilkins grew a small herd of horses into the massive Wilkins Horse Ranch. Her older son, Johnny, tended the horses; her younger son, Sam, managed the bookkeeping; and her daughter, Kitty, marketed their horse crop. Later known as the "Horse Queen of Idaho," Kitty would travel to horse markets across the Midwest to meet with buyers. The buyers were primarily army procurement officers purchasing remounts for the cavalry.

Kitty was beautiful, talented, and intelligent. She was trained at the finest finishing school in the West. When negotiating prices for her horses, Kitty often dazzled procurement officers with her beauty and charm, and then she used her wit to outmatch them.

As the automobile became more popular and the cavalry switched from horses to a more mechanized army, the fortunes of the Wilkins Horse Ranch faded. In a tragic ending, Kitty died October 8, 1936, alone and penniless. But her notoriety and legacy in Southwestern Idaho remains almost mythic.

About the author...

Gus Brackett grew up on a working cattle ranch in the wide-open spaces of Southwestern Idaho and Northeastern Nevada. He began riding horses at age five and sold his first steer at age ten. As a child, Gus attended a one-room schoolhouse, where he started writing stories about cowboys.

Gus first heard tall tales about early cowboys from Grandpa Noy Brackett, Uncle Rolly Patrick, and Truman Clark. These stories fascinated Gus. So, in 2010, he began to chronicle them in his Badger Thurston series. In 2020, Gus began adding to the collection with this Nettie McCorkle book, the first in a sister series he is developing.

Gus currently lives and works on the same ranch he grew up on. And he's chairman of the board of that one-room schoolhouse. He, his wife, Kimberly, and their four children live in a little ranch house, and they have a barn full of horses, steers, dogs, cats, and chickens.

Badger Thurston is an ordinary kid in 1910. But a simple job can turn dangerous in troubled times.

By Gus Brackett
Illustrations by Don Gill

When the foreman is pushed into the mud pit, Badger is named as a suspect. With the help of his old friend Percy and a new friend Eliyah, Badger searches far and wide for clues…with an angry mob chasing him. Does the mob catch Badger or does he find the culprit and clear his name?

Read Badger Thurston and the Mud Pits to find out.

Badger Thurston and the Mud Pit is the third in an exciting series of adventures specifically designed for adventurous kids. The Badger Thurston series is action packed and easy reading. Every book is less than eight chapters with illustrations to hold every readers attention

Look for Badger Thurston on Amazon.com and follow Badger Thurston on Facebook.
For more information e-mail the author at
12bookbaskets@gmail.com

Badger Thurston is an ordinary teen in 1910. But sometimes ordinary teens do extraordinary things, like riding in his first rodeo with the best cowboy in the area, Charlie Pickett.

Only days into his new job, Badger comes nose to nose with some unfriendly characters who want the young cowboy to hightail it away from the rodeo. Why are the bullies pushing Badger to clear off? And will he decide to leave the ropin', ridin' and brandin' behind?

Badger Thurston and the Trouble at the Rodeo is the fourth in an exciting series of adventures specifically designed for adventurous kids. The Badger Thurston series is action packed and easy to read. Every book is eight chapters with illustrations to keep every reader's attention.

Look for Badger Thurston on Amazon.com and follow Badger Thurston on Facebook.
For more information e-mail the author at
12bookbaskets@gmail.com

Have you been looking for a series of books you can share with the whole family? How about a novel that sparks your child's interest in the Old West? The Badger Thurston series is a series of novels for a youth audience that follows life in 1910. The stories are fast paced enough to appeal to today's child, but still true to the history of the intermountain area. The series is sprinkled with humor and action that will hold the attention of all readers.

Badger Thurston is written by Gus Brackett and contains seven illustrations by renowned cowboy artist Don Gill. Any of the books in the Badger Thurston series would be a great addition to any family library.

Ask about our "Badger in every library" program to donate copies of Badger Thurston to your local school or library.

See what the toughest critics have said about "Badger Thurston and the Cattle Drive:"

"I thought it was funny. I loved the book very much."
Kodee S., age 10

Look for Badger Thurston on Amazon.com and follow Badger Thurston on Facebook.
For more information e-mail the author at
12bookbaskets@gmail.com

If you enjoyed this book, then you will enjoy the books in the Badger Thurston series. It's the year 1910. Badger Thurston is an ordinary kid, but trouble seems to find him wherever he goes...as a cowboy, as a teamster, and as a flunkie on a construction site.

The Badger Thurston books will be enjoyed by the whole family. Action, adventure, mystery...these easy reading books will spark your interest in the Old West.

Badger Thurston and the Cattle Drive
Badger Thurston and the Runaway Stagecoach
Badger Thurston and the Mud Pits
Badger Thurston and the Trouble at the Rodeo

Watch for the next book in this series.

Order your copy today at:
www.badgerthurston.com or on **Amazon.com**.

Or send a check or money order for $10.25 plus $3.50 for shipping and handling to:

12 Baskets Book Publishing
54899 Crawfish Rd.
Rogerson ID 83302

www.ingramcontent.com/pod-product-compliance
Lightning Source LLC
Chambersburg PA
CBHW071412170626
46811CB00003B/1373